PASS the BOTTLE

PASS the BOTTLE
Rum Tales of the West Coast

ERIC NEWSOME

ORCA BOOK PUBLISHERS

Cataloguing in Publication Data
Newsome, Eric, 1925 -
Pass the Bottle

Includes bibliographic references and index.
ISBN 1-55143-044-4
1. Prohibition–Pacific Coast (U.S.)–History. 2. Prohibition–British Columbia–History. 3. Smuggling–Pacific Coast (U.S.)–History.
4. Smuggling–British Columbia–History. I. Title.
HV5090.P2N48 1995   364.1'33   C95-910445-3

We gratefully acknowledge the financial support of the Canada Council

Cover design by Christine Toller
Cover illustration by Roy Schneider
Printed and bound in Canada

Orca Book Publishers
PO Box 5626, Station B
Victoria, BC Canada
V8R 6S4

Orca Book Publishers
PO Box 468
Custer, WA USA
98240-0468

10   9   8   7   6   5   4   3   2   1

For
Nigel and Marielle,
Alissa and Chantal

CONTENTS

1
CATCH AS CATCH CAN

If ever you travel along the Oregon coast, pause at Whale Cove and search carefully along the shore. With luck, you might find an old bottle buried in the sand. With greater luck, the bottle's contents might be intact. Not many years ago, an encrusted bottle was found there, unharmed, tightly corked, and full. According to a cautious taster, the well-aged whisky had lost none of its potency.

There is a link between the possibility of finding such a bottle and the presence of nearby Smuggler's Rock. How could it be otherwise? And both bottle and rock are linked to the shipwreck of a Canadian rumrunner. In total they form part of a prohibition-day's yarn in which an illicit liquor cargo turned out to be too slippery to hold and the vessel's crew almost impossible for the police to lose.

Looking back on their rumrunning careers, Charles Ryall, William Kerr and Stanley Babcock would remember February 7, 1932, without much effort. It was the date of the shipwreck that had followed a normal departure from home on a mission that was outwardly no different from many others, but which had almost cost them their lives.

On the first day of February, the trio cast off, turned the nose of their thirty-six-foot powerboat away from the city lights of Victoria, British Columbia, and quietly motored out into the Strait of Georgia.

There was nothing unusual about their going. Similar boats moved in and out of the harbour night and day. And, given the time and place, the *Sea Island*'s cargo—three thousand gallons of high-grade liquor destined for a Portland liquor baron—would have raised few eyebrows. If there was a difference in the boat's mission, it lay in the fact that the cargo was to be landed directly on shore by the Canadian crew, rather than being transferred at sea to an American boat for the final run in.

A week after leaving Victoria, the *Sea Island* lay rolling in a heavy swell some way off the Oregon coast: far enough away not to be easily visible to prying watchers on the shore, but near enough to be able to get to its planned landfall with no time wasted. The crew members were exhausted. For seven days they had dealt with winds that ranged from gusty to gale force, had ridden the light chop of sheltered waters, bucketed along in seas of a sterner variety, and glissaded down the steep slopes of cresting waves. The Pacific Ocean, they called it! To the weary men, there was nothing pacific about it. But they were sure the worst was over. Soon they would rest. And, even better, soon they would be well paid for a successful voyage and head home to live like kings for as long as the money lasted.

As darkness fell, the *Sea Island* turned and ran for shore. The ocean swells, dead on her stern, caught and lifted her. Each crest hurled her forward, and then, lagging behind the wave, she slid down its back to wallow in a deep, watery trough. It was a wild roller-coaster ride, made worse by the blindfold of night. But once shallower water was reached, the wave action took on a shorter, steeper pitch, foam flecked the surface, and the boom of breaking waves filled the air. The sailors peered forward uneasily, straining their eyes into the blackness.

"There they are. Ten degrees to starboard."

"Where?"

"There!"

The helmsman picked out two dim lights, one set above the other, signaling that the coast was clear. They also acted as lead-in lights and pointed out the direction of the deep channel that led to the sheltered waters of Whale Cove.

This was the tricky part.

The helmsman altered course slightly. Now the breaking waves were hurling the boat forward, but also pushing her slightly off course.

The men on board were stiff with tension. They anxiously searched the heaving waters for the dark shapes of rocks.

"Watch out! Rock to port." The urgent cry twisted in the wind.

If the helmsman heard the call, it was too late. As the warning was given, a cresting wave lifted the boat and crashed it into a boulder at the end of the reef on the south side of the entrance to Whale Cove. Smuggler's Rock had got its name.

The *Sea Island* was finished. Salt water poured through a hole in her hull and she sank in the shallows near the shore. The worst was over, or so her crew had thought. And now this. They struggled to shore and staggered up the beach, soaking wet and chilled to the bone by the brisk February wind.

Their predicament went beyond that of mere discomfort. Three Canadians without official permission to land were stranded on an Oregon beach, and the remains of their boat was loaded with evidence of an attempt to thwart American prohibition laws.

But they were not alone. From the shelter of the tall trees in which the lead-in lanterns had been hung, men of the shore party rushed to the beach to help. The smugglers were wet. That was of no concern. They would all be wet before this lot was over. The important thing was to save the liquor and get it hidden before the prohibition agents got wind of the wreck. The bootleggers had a temporary advantage; the night was dark, the meeting place had been a well-kept secret, and the coast was lonely. They worked like demons and started to get the liquor hidden.

The distinguishing marks on the *Sea Island* were obliterated, and then, to be doubly sure that she would be untraceable, she was set on fire. Evidence of liquor smuggling was going to be hard to find.

When most of the liquor was safely hidden, Ryall, Babcock and Kerr were taken care of. All the other men involved had good reason to be where they were; the shipwrecked trio had not. They would have to quietly disappear. Given a car, they were started out in the general direction of Portland. Once there, the brains of the rumrunning conspiracy would get them back into Canada. Crossing borders secretly was their business.

The coast road was dark, twisting and lonely, the car unfamiliar. All three rumrunners were exhausted. Seven days on a rough sea, a shipwreck, and the hard work of helping to hide the liquor had made sure of that. The driver missed a turn, and the car ended up on its side in a deep ditch. And there it stayed. A shipwreck closely followed by a car crash! The dispirited men made their way on foot to the nearest town and waited for a bus to Portland, all the while trying to be inconspicuous. After a cold wait, they boarded the bus, flopped down on comfortable seats, stretched out in the unaccustomed warmth, and enjoyed the feeling that their troubles were over.

When a police officer inspected the wrecked car the next morning, he found that it had been reported stolen. The hunt was on. A few questions around town identified three likely suspects. Where were they? On a bus to Portland, as far as anyone knew. But they might have got off anywhere along the route. The officer checked his watch. The bus would just about be arriving in Portland. Had they stayed on the bus, there was still a chance that the three men could be picked up for questioning. A slim chance. A phone call to Portland had police officers rushing down to the bus station. The bus was in—and empty. A taxi was about to leave. The officers shouted to the driver to hold it and rushed over. Stanley Babcock, Charles Ryall and William Kerr had no chance to escape. They were bundled out of the taxicab and placed under arrest.

Back in Whale Cove, events had not turned out as planned. The shore gang, having buried most of the *Sea Island*'s cargo in the sands, was spotted by the authorities. The men immediately scattered and hid in the woods until they could make their separate ways home.

It was a star-crossed operation. Within hours a local newspaper reported that almost three thousand gallons of contraband liquor had been dug up by the authorities and immediately destroyed. No one could quibble about the speed of reporting, but the accuracy of the news left something to be desired. In fact, the liquor had been confiscated by the Lincoln County sheriff, trucked to Toledo, and stored in the Lincoln County jail. So all that had been found was locked up—safely locked up, the sheriff presumed. But not all the cargo had been found. Three weeks later the sheriff got his hands on another fourteen cases of whisky. And that was still not all. When summer rolled around, Whale Cove became a popular picnic area—pleasant and with a chance of a liquid find to make one's day.

The efforts made to hide the identity of the *Sea Island* failed.

The best efforts of Ryall, Kerr and Babcock to disassociate themselves from the wreck also failed. And when they finally admitted that they had been the *Sea Island*'s crew, their protestations that she had not been carrying contraband liquor brought only a smile from their captors. It was, said Ryall, a simple fishing trip. Their engine had failed and they had drifted into the cove. As a last resort the anchor had been dropped but it had failed to hold, and the *Sea Island* had been tossed onto a spine of rock by the heavy seas and had spontaneously burst into flames. They had managed to row to shore in the skiff and thought themselves lucky to be alive.

The wrecked car was easily explained. A motorist passing along the road by the cove where they had landed had been kind enough to offer them a lift. Unfortunately he had lost control of the car and overturned it in a ditch. Again they had been fortunate to escape injury and from that point on had trusted themselves to the professional skills of a bus driver. They had no idea where the driver of the car had gone. The police were far from impressed; as far as they were concerned, the trio could tell it to the judge.

The three Canadian seamen were a minor part of a large business organization that had suffered an unacceptable loss. And recovery of the loss was possible. But what they needed to put things straight—their confiscated liquor—was locked in an Oregon jail. The solution was obvious: jails had been broken out of often enough; they would pull a switch and break in.

It was a Sunday in late March and just after midnight when a small convoy of vehicles, lights off, pulled up outside the darkened county jail in Toledo. For once, the jail held no prisoners, and that meant no custodial staff on duty. The coast was as clear as it would ever be. The plan of attack had been well rehearsed. As a large sedan stopped, men with guns drawn piled out and moved silently to seal off the area. At the same time, the doors of a stylish coupe swung open, and two men, both wearing long overcoats and wide-brimmed hats that set them apart from the rest of the rough-looking crew, got out. No words were necessary. The taller of the men pointed to a truck drawn across the front of the building and with a gesture started a group of men carrying a heavy metal contraption towards the solid jailhouse door. The solidity was deceptive. One man bent to the lock, inserted a tool, twisted, and the door opened. So much for breaking into jails. There were other locks and other minor pauses to deal with them, and then there was a bigger problem. The liquor they had come to remove became visible in the shaded pencil beams of flashlights—well out of reach and piled against the stone outer wall of a heavily barred cell. The cell lock, set in a framework of solid iron bars, was beyond picking. But no matter. Within seconds the metal contraption was wheeled up, and a thickset man put on protective goggles and got to work. A turned cylinder valve brought a hiss of gas, and a deftly applied spark brought a roaring jet of flame. The operator touched the tip of the flame to the bars surrounding the lock, and one by one they glowed, dripped molten gobs of iron, and parted. From outside, the guards looked nervously towards the jailhouse where the windows showed a flickering light. This was the dangerous time and they gripped their guns tightly. But the town slept, and no dogs barked.

Soon the last bar holding the cell lock parted, and the lock fell to the floor with a clang. With his leather-gloved hand, the operator pushed against the hot metal of the cell door and it swung open. Problem solved.

"Move it, guys." The shorter of the well-dressed men spoke the first words since the vehicles had drawn to a halt outside.

And move it they did. In a remarkably short time, the sacking-wrapped bundles heaped in the cell were stowed on the two trucks and the convoy moved inland. It had been a smooth operation and the participants were jubilant. Perhaps unwisely so.

An hour's journey from the coast one truck ran out of gas. That was easily fixed. The second truck pulled up alongside and siphoning began. But while the gas transfer was taking the truckers' attention, police cars arrived and took them by surprise. It was an unequal contest. Speedily, the truck crews were disarmed, handcuffed and bundled into backup police cars. Without haste, the police officers examined the trucks' cargoes and showed no surprise at what they found. Someone had quietly sung a little song. Only the timing was off. On their way to catch the jailbreakers in the act, the police had missed the main event but caught up with the action in its second stage.

There was unfinished business to be attended to. The trucks set off in the direction of Portland again, but this time with police drivers and crews. Not far down the road, men from a sedan parked by the road waved the trucks down.

Again the surprise element caught the bandits unprepared. The four men already under arrest were soon joined by three more from the sedan. So far, seven Americans, known to be implicated in Portland liquor smuggling rings, had been arrested. But there was more. Three more men found in the back seat of the sedan were advised to step out slowly while steadily aimed police revolvers gave encouragement. Hands held high, they staggered out: Charles Ryall, William Kerr and Stanley Babcock, Canadian citizens all.

The police had enjoyed more success than was their usual lot. Ten men were under arrest and would be charged with the destruction of public property, the theft of government evidence, and transporting and having in possession, while armed, alcoholic beverages in violation of the national Prohibition Act. That lot would take some dodging! But a loose end remained. Where was the stylish coupe and its well-dressed occupants? That remained an unsolved mystery. The common soldiers of the rum trade had been taken; the generals who plotted, planned and took the lion's share of the profits had, as usual, escaped. For them there would be no punishment.

The Canadians, on the other hand, were due an extra ration of grief. To the array of charges they faced in common with their American friends would be added one of smuggling. Out on bail while that matter was being prepared for prosecution, they had used their freedom to add to their sins against Andrew Volstead's law.

The tides of American temperance and outright prohibition of strong drink had ebbed and flowed for much of the country's history. The tavern was evil and must go. The evil was real: the violence of reformers, attacking taverns with irons bars and axes, seemed little better. Alcoholic drink led to moral decay, disease and death. A drinking scale, starting with punch as a cause of idleness, gaming, sickness and debt and advancing through gin, brandy and rum as the precursors of burglary, murder, madness, despair and the gallows, was firmly believed by some and mocked by others. Immorality relating to drunkenness was in need of control. The religious had no qualms about imposing their views on others. With the beginning of the First World War, it became fashionably patriotic not to drink alcoholic beverages. But the engulfing wave was yet to come. After the war ended, in a wash of religious zeal, total prohibition was proposed for the entire United States. Remarkably, the proposal passed and the Volstead Act became law. In Norfolk, Virginia, evangelist Billy Sunday praised the Lord and, in a mock burial service, consigned to his grave John Barleycorn, symbol of strong drink. Poor John was dead and gone. America was dry. The chance of alcoholic drink flooding the land again was no more likely than Barleycorn's resurrection. But that was a subject on which there were conflicting opinions.

Ryall, Babcock and Kerr escaped the full punishment due for their Oregon smuggling escapade. Thirteen years had passed since the advent of total prohibition and the world had changed. Prohibition in its turn was about to die as John Barleycorn had died.

But had John Barleycorn died? Not at all. What the law would not allow, evaders of the law had kept on supplying. The "noble experiment" of total prohibition failed miserably. Attempts to apply the law had cost dearly; two hundred and fifty men—enforcers and evaders—were dead. That had not been intended when prohibition had quietly taken the stage. Neither had it been intended that between 1920 and 1933 over forty-five thousand American citizens would find access to liquor so easy that they would die of alcoholism.

Such men as the crew of the *Sea Island* helped the unfortunates to die. Legally, in the eyes of Canadian law, they were pure as the driven snow. For citizens of the United States, it was a different matter; the law they were breaking was that of their own country. Morality mattered not at all. There was lots of money to be made—easy money. There was an appeal to the adventurous spirit of those bored by the prosaic pattern of normal life. There was reason enough to smuggle rum—the generic term for all forms of banned alcoholic drink—and, in so doing, the rumrunners wrote a fascinating chapter in the history of the west coast of North America.

2
JUST A BUSINESS?

The air above the waters of Brown's Bay, Washington, was distinctly cool as a group of silent men unloaded a cargo of smuggled Canadian liquor from a tugboat close inshore. With hours of concealing darkness still to come, the men believed themselves to be in no danger of discovery. But darkness is neutral. If it hid them, it could hide others.

And it did. From the cover of a nearby wood, silent men were watching and waiting. When the unloading was done, they would move. It would be far easier to grab the illicit cargo of liquor once it was all safely on shore. The greater the weight of evidence taken, the greater would be the certainty of a conviction.

As the last of the burlap-wrapped bottles came ashore, the unloading party relaxed. The hard work was over. All that remained was to get the cargo to Seattle by road. Buyers for the liquor would not be hard to find.

And then all hell broke loose. Lights shone from the woods and illuminated the men on the beach in stark relief. Voices called on them to throw down their weapons and raise their hands. Confused, some did and some did not. A volley of shots kicked sand up around the feet of the reluctant and persuaded them to obey.

Then a car engine roared, and a dark shape sped along the road,

Burlap-wrapped bottles on their way to ease dry American throats.
(photo courtesy of the Coast Guard Museum, Seattle)

away from the beach, towards safety. The ambushing party had anticipated something of the kind and had taken precautions. Almost too late, the driver of the car saw the roadblock. With a desperate wrench on the wheel he headed for the bushes at the side of the road. The car bucked over the uneven ground, spraying great gouts of loose soil behind its madly spinning wheels. Branches clawed at the paintwork. More shots rang out. The driver, head down, saw the end of the roadblock hurtle by and twisted the car back onto the road. The hubbub fell far behind. He was out. He was away. Clean away. The driver slowed. There was no point in drawing attention to himself. The wild ride around the roadblock had no doubt left its mark on the car, but such damage was easily fixed. Whatever repairs were needed could be done quickly and quietly. There was nothing to connect him to the failed liquor smuggling attempt. Perhaps some of his men had been caught. That was too bad, but not dangerous. He paid them too well to entertain the notion of betrayal.

Later in the day, a police car pulled up outside a Seattle house. Police officers walked up the path, and one rapped on the front door. When the owner of the house opened the door, the officers seemed oddly deferential. He was, they said, under arrest for involvement in liquor smuggling. True to protocol, an officer read him his rights. It was not really necessary. Roy Olmstead, lieutenant in the Seattle Police Department, knew all about rights. His escape from Brown's Bay had not been as clean as he had imagined; one of the prohibition agents at the ambush had identified him as the speeding driver.

Olmstead started out as a shipyard worker and then, at the age of twenty, joined the Seattle Police Department. He was a good cop, hard-working, ambitious and intelligent; a man expected to go far in the police hierarchy. After four years' service, he was a sergeant; after ten years, a lieutenant—the youngest the department had ever appointed. Roy Olmstead's police years were spent in interesting times. Seattle was a growing city, volatile in politics and violent in nature. And state-wide liquor prohibition was no help to the police—except, perhaps, as an aid to the practical education of Lieutenant Olmstead. He watched, acted for law and order, and learned. The rumrunning gangs were inefficient and made up of men more comfortable with violence than productive thought. Olmstead thought them stupid.

In 1920, American politicians blanketed the entire nation with a prohibition commandment: thou shalt not manufacture, sell, barter, transport, import, export, deliver, or furnish any intoxicating liquor. It was a comprehensive ban. In theory, the United States was a huge island of drought set in the midst of an ocean of strong drink. But many citizens, already restive under the original ten commandments, smiled. Go thirsty? Never! Prohibition by states had not worked, and prohibition on a national scale would have even less chance of success.

In frontier days, what could not be bought could be made— liquor included. And that proud pioneer tradition lived on. If prohibition had dried up the well, a well of another sort could be profitably dug. There was always moonshine to be had. But a drinker of moonshine was taking a chance. Only the barest knowledge of distilling was needed for liquor production. The ingredients were cheap and easy to obtain. Sugar, water and yeast made up the mash. That and garbage—whatever was to hand. "The more juicy the garbage, the better the mash and the better the shine," moonshiners claimed. Hygiene was a word, not a necessity. It played no part in the process.

Industrial alcohol was also available. To avoid misuse, the law required that an unpalatable ingredient be included in the alcohol manufacturing process to make it undrinkable. It was included, but unscrupulous suppliers met the demand for alcoholic drink by disguising the foul taste with extra ingredients. But how safe was the resulting devil's brew? Not safe at all. Desperate drinkers tried it, and many died for their sins. To the dry zealots bereft of compassion, death was a fitting punishment for trying to evade the prohibition laws they so ardently supported.

But there was another way to drink. Roy Olmstead's way. Dismissed from the force and fined a mere $500 for his Brown's Bay escapade, he went into full-time rumrunning—"the respectable crime." In a market awash with watered-down products, toxic moonshine and industrial alcohol, he vowed to sell only name-brand liquor at full strength. Smuggling apart, his men would act with decorum. Investment of profits in gambling and prostitution was not to be considered. He was, a newspaper approvingly reported, a good bootlegger, "in many ways the best thing that could have happened in the Northwest." Many Seattle residents agreed and idolized him as a popular hero.

For Olmstead it was just a business. Those with a fondness for liquor were unlikely to lose that fondness by decree and would continue to demand the drink of their choice. Somehow, suppliers would meet their wishes. Demand had always called forth supply. It always would. That was the foundation of American business life. And, if home supplies were lacking, imports would fill the gap. That also was natural enough.

Clearly, Canada had great advantages as a potential supplier. Although far from free to drink as they wished, Canadians had not banned the production of liquors for export. Such a ban would have made no sense. Why kill a prosperous industry?

The land border between Canada and the United States of America was of such a length as to make efficient policing impossible. To the west, the forty-ninth parallel of latitude, straight as a die from just west of Lake Superior to the Pacific shore, went berserk when it hit salt water. Part way across the Strait of Georgia, the border cut a jagged course between a tight scattering of islands before neatly bisecting the Strait of Juan de Fuca and ending at the outer limit of territorial waters. The border leaked and the leakage was transformed as it flowed. Liquor passing from Canada to the United States was legal and became illegal, was cheap and became expensive. Those assisting the flow could hardly avoid becoming rich.

And almost anyone could get involved. All it took was a boat, a handful of dollars to buy liquor, and the guts to land the contraband on United States shores in defiance of national prohibition laws. Smuggling was not new on the west coast. In the past, illicit trade in playing cards, sugar, wool, opium and anything else that could earn a few dollars—even Chinese immigrants, when they had been barred from legal entry—had established a smuggling tradition. There was no shortage of willing volunteers to spark a revival by carrying liquor. But much of the traffic was carried out by small men dealing in small quantities.

Roy Olmstead was not interested in small quantities. He had huge liquor cargoes shipped from Canada's westcoast ports and, safely in international waters, siphoned them off into small boats that headed for the Washington shore not many miles south of the Canadian ports of origin. His shipments flooded the Seattle liquor market, and in the best of times his monthly liquor deals were valued at $250,000. Just a business, as he had claimed, but a huge business.

All this led to Olmstead becoming one of Seattle's largest employers. Office workers and rumrunning crews, dispatchers and checkers, salesmen and warehousemen, all had good reason to thank him for their daily bread. And so had a large number of men who were supposedly employed as guardians of American moral values but who were paid to be blind when rumrunning operations were under way. Dealing in large quantities of smuggled liquor made it possible for Olmstead to undercut the street prices charged by his competitors. Who will pay dearly when the same product is on offer more cheaply? The Seattle market became his near monopoly. The king of Puget Sound rumrunners was highly respected. His circle of friends was large. He encouraged science and the arts. His purchase of a mansion in a fashionable residential area demonstrated his business success. Admirers crowded round him, anxious to be seen with so great a man. It was good to be a rumrunner.

But if rumrunning was only a business to Roy Olmstead it was much more than that to the United States Coast Guard, first

Question: why should a bollard be removable? *(photo courtesy of the Coast Guard Museum, Seattle)*

defense against smugglers. The organization, brought into being to fight smugglers of rum from the Caribbean to the populated Atlantic coast at the end of the eighteenth century, had deteriorated over time, and when prohibition became the law of the land, the coast guard motto—*Semper Paratus* (Always Ready)—was more of a mockery than a promise. By then, its ships were few, old and slow; its sailors, a rag-tag bunch collected from around the seven seas, were more experienced in chasing the demon rum for its anticipated delights than in apprehending rumrunners. Taken individually, the crew members were good sailors; collectively, they had a language problem that made efficiency impossible. An officer of the coast guard ship *Tampa* complained that her mainly foreign-

Answer: to get at the filler cap of a hidden liquor tank. *(photo courtesy of the Coast Guard Museum, Seattle)*

born crew understood twenty-five different languages but understood simple English with the greatest of difficulty. American-born men seemed not to have been attracted to a service that had a dreary police function as its reason for existence.

But, whatever the state of men and equipment, the coast guard had an impossible task. The island of drought that was the United States had endless miles of sea-washed shore. Too much to watch. Too much to handle if it could be watched. On the Atlantic coast, a motley rum fleet rode at anchor in plain view of the towers of New York City. This was where Bill McCoy, a rum dealer who supplied only the best-quality drink, gave his name to all that was genuine and good—"the real McCoy." This was where traders from the shore made daily visits to take orders for anything that the ships' crews required: fresh food, daily newspapers, entertainers and even prostitutes if the price was right. Secure in international waters, the rum-boat crews thumbed their noses at the watching coast guard. Watching was easy, doing something about what was seen was a different story. Night after night, a sunset fleet of speedboats left the shore to load liquor from their chosen supply ship and then, shielded by darkness, favoured by speed, and in numbers too great for interception to be likely, raced back to shore. Night after night, coast guard commanders were left fuming in impotent rage.

New York City, densely populated and lively, had a thirst for liquor that made for a densely populated Rum Row. On the thinly populated Pacific fringe, where smaller cities were separated by many miles of empty ˈshore, rumrunning was a lonelier affair and Rum Row was harder to define and harder to find. Any success the coast guard detachments would achieve would be in confined coastal waters rather than on the open ocean.

Such a confined hunting ground was Puget Sound, the domain of Chief Boatswain Lorenz A. Lonsdale, commander of the coast guard ship *Arcata*. "Grandad," as he was known to friends and enemies alike, was small in stature—just five feet tall—and large in reputation. His ship was old and ugly. On her low hull sat a long, many-windowed deck-house that stood tall and stretched from the short forward deck almost to the stern. On the forward end of the deck-house, and adding to the overall impression of height, was perched a small wheel-house. To complete the *Arcata*'s top-heavy look, air scoops rose to a level higher than the deck-house roof, and a single funnel, braced by guy-wires, rose high above all. When the skinny funnel was painting the sky with its inkiest pall, the ship's single propeller might, with luck, be pushing her through the water at a modest twelve knots. On the forward deck was mounted a cannon. The cannon could hurl one-pound shells to a maximum distance of four thousand yards, but with wild inaccuracy. At five hundred yards it was more accurate, but the problem lay in getting the gun close enough to a suspicious boat to make effective use of its short-range accuracy. The rumrunners, with unlawful profits to burn, could buy boats fast enough to keep out of range and take advantage of every improvement in engine technology. The coast guard, relying on the crumbs of financing provided by politicians, made do with what they had and watched helplessly as the performance gap between pursued and pursuers widened.

The coast guard cutter *Arcata*. No match for speedy rumrunners.
(photo courtesy of the Coast Guard Museum, Seattle)

But speed and force was not always required—panic helped. Checking Deception Pass at the northern end of Whidbey Island, Lonsdale ordered a heavily laden boat to stop. It did—eventually, and in an unexpected way. Hitting the throttle wide open, her helmsman responded to the order by racing for the shore at high speed and beaching his craft. Then smoke rose as the frustrated rumrunner set his boat on fire, after which he rapidly disappeared into the nearby woods with his companion. By the time the *Arcata*'s dinghy had reached the shore, the burning boat was beyond saving. But there was some cause for celebration. Six cases of liquor had survived; proof of law breaking that led to a conviction when the fleeing men were later caught.

And if panic could catch rumrunners, so could fog—if the gods were being kind. Anchored off Marrowstone Point in a depressingly thick fog, "Grandad" Lonsdale found that he had company. Faintly visible through the murk was a boat with a rakish look. A boarding party visited and returned with twenty-four cases of illicit booze. Not a lot, but enough to give a thrill of accomplishment to a coast guard crew who saw far too many retreating and untouchable sterns disappearing towards the horizon.

In another liquor confiscation, luck once more played a major role. A self-serving official report told how the rumrunners had been arrested by the coast guard while landing a cargo on a beach on San Juan Island. A Friday Harbor newspaper told it differently. Its pages revealed that the rumrunners—boat, cargo and all—had been stranded on a reef for two days and were delighted to see the coast guard. It was a rescue rather than a police action as claimed. Unkindly, the newspaper editor added the comment that the incident was the first coast guard success in nine months.

Finding clear evidence of rumrunning was a rare occurrence. If capture seemed likely, the rumrunner's crew immediately started to dump the liquor overboard. Dumping brought loss but failing to dump brought a greater loss, that of the boat and the freedom of the crew. There were times when Lonsdale examined boats from which illicit cargoes had recently been ejected to sink to the sea floor. The rumrunners knew that they had been smuggling and so did Lonsdale, but what could he do about it? Nothing, as far as the law went. But he invariably stood before his captives, looking like a small enraged rooster, and lectured them severely on the error of their ways, while wagging an admonishing finger under their noses. Once he had made his point, the captor and his captives parted, the *Arcata* to continue her career of frustration, the rumrunners to drag the seabed in the hope of recovering their jettisoned cargo.

One thing was clear: the coast guard was making a scarcely appreciable dent in the business affairs of illicit liquor distributors such as Roy Olmstead. And if times were good for Olmstead, they were even better for his suppliers across the border in Canada. Smuggled liquor originated where it must, but Canadian businessmen had a huge locational advantage. On hearing of the prohibition amendment, they rudely remarked on its proof of American insanity, rolled up their sleeves, and prepared to meet the demands of a lucrative market from which all home-based suppliers had been removed at the stroke of a pen.

Canadian distillers, producing alcoholic drinks in huge quantities and selling to whoever wished to buy, were in a seller's heaven. On their home ground they would sell to anyone, and where the product went after the sale lost them no sleep. A member of the Bronfman distilling family, owners of Seagram's, made the point. "We loaded carloads of goods, got our money, and shipped it . . . I never went to the other side of the border to count the empty Seagram's bottles."

Supply on the west coast could never catch up with demand. To the stream of Canadian liquor passing through the ports of Vancouver and Victoria was added a river of foreign liquor, stored in bonded warehouses until required.

Naturally, the Canadian government wanted a share in the profits and decreed that an export duty of $20 on each case of liquor should be imposed. Imposed for a certain destination, that is. Almost without exception, exported liquor went to the United States—everybody knew that. The trifling amount of money to be raised by duty on exports to other countries was not worth the trouble of collecting. That being so, liquor declared destined for the United States was dutiable while liquor for any other destination sailed duty-free. That liquor could not legally enter the United States was not a consideration. The Canadian decision was as pragmatic as it was unwise. In the real world it made no sense for Canadian exporters to declare the United States as a destination when naming any other destination in the world would avoid the necessity to pay duty. By its export duty policy, the Canadian government shaped the rum trade.

On the west coast, liquor orders for the United States were loaded on ocean-going ships and a port in another country named as the destination. In international waters the ship came to rest. There, on Rum Row, small boats took as many bottles as they could safely carry from the mother ship and headed for shore— American boats directly; Canadian boats usually for secret places among the Gulf Islands where a transfer was made to fast American speedboats which took the liquor ashore. It was an effective operation that gave steady business to Canadian shipping firms and brought fame of a sort to many of those involved.

One of the Canadian shipping industry's leading lights on the west coast was a one-time farmer. Charles H. Hudson was not a very good farmer. The work was hard, the hours long and the rewards poor. In fact, when Hudson shook the prairie dust from his shoes and headed west for the coast he had suffered four years of financial loss. Once established in Vancouver, a recommendation given to him by the police chief of Winnipeg led him to a local sealing captain who offered him a job on the *Borealis*. Hudson knew nothing of sealing, but it sounded better than trying to grow crops on dry interior plains. It paid better too. After what he later described as a six-day pleasure cruise, and never a seal in sight, $400 was slipped into his hand as wages. It seemed too good to be true. But it was true. Charles Hudson, late of His Majesty's Royal Navy, recipient of the Distinguished Service Cross and Bar for bravery at sea in World War I, had returned to the sea. He had stumbled into a job that not only paid well but added zest to his life. Accidentally, he had become a member of the rumrunning fraternity. When the *Borealis* had left Vancouver with him on board, her holds had carried a thousand cases of liquor towards a delivery rendezvous with an American vessel. When she returned, her holds were empty. It was a long time since the *Borealis* had caught a seal.

Rising rapidly from the position of casual crew member and rookie rumrunner, Charles Hudson became marine superintendent of Consolidated Exporters and, some claimed, the mastermind of the Pacific version of Rum Row. Participation in an activity that poured illegal liquor into the United States brought Hudson no qualms of conscience. What he did brought money to westcoast ports, gave seamen work, and operated within Canadian laws. He claimed to have been happy as a link in a chain that supplied good liquor to thirsty Americans and kept them from poisoning themselves with rotten moonshine. Perhaps he had a point; an estimate suggested the presence of ten thousand illegal stills in Washington State alone when national prohibition began in 1920. Lacking a source of the real thing, it was a number that would inevitably grow.

Unfortunately, the careers of Captain Hudson and many others in the rum trade are matters of conjecture rather than of certainty. Fraser Miles, author of *Slow Boat on Rum Row*, writing of a business in which he took part, bemoaned the fate of those wishing to write of the doings of men who "made the sphinx sound like a chatterbox." Men who unswervingly followed the precept, "Don't never tell nobody nothing, nohow." Men who, if questioned directly, never gave an answer of any relevance—if they answered at all. Most of what is known of Captain Hudson comes from Ruth Greene's *Personality Ships of British Columbia* and is based on her interviews with him. Fraser Miles expressed surprise that she got so much information. He, an old-time rumrunner and previous acquaintance, when interviewing the aging captain, could get no more than a mumbled repetition of the words, "And nobody ever talked."

If the rumrunners were tight-lipped and parsimonious with spoken words, it follows that few left any written record of their affairs. And yet all commercial vessels had to keep a log. The logs of many rumrunning ships are still to be found in dusty archives: circumspect documents, bland and untrue. Rumrunning skippers kept two logs—one official and one unofficial. The long-lost un-official logs told the truth. They were the logs kept in weighted bags during rumrunning expeditions and kept handy for hurling over the side if it seemed that capture was imminent.

There it was. Supply and demand; salesmen and customers; ordering, shipping and distributing. Just a business, as Roy Olmstead had claimed. And far from the west coast there was an-other big operator who took the modest businessman tack. Conveniently ignoring the host of serious crimes associated with his activities, Al Capone said, "I make my money by supplying a public demand. If I break the law, my customers, who number hundreds of the best people in Chicago, are as guilty as I am. The only difference between us is that I sell and they buy. Every-body calls me a racketeer. I call myself a businessman. When I sell liquor, it's bootlegging. When my patrons serve it on a silver tray on Lakeshore Drive, it's hospitality."

But the United States Coast Guard had shown itself not to be unduly impressed by such businessmen, and the Prohibition Bureau, newly formed to police the land side of rumrunning, seemed set to take the same view. Not that it mattered much what it thought: to the rum trade the bureau was a joke; to the public, a cesspool of inefficiency and corruption.

The figures told the story. To keep a nation-wide force of twenty-three hundred agents employed, the Bureau made over eighteen thousand appointments in its first eleven years of exis-tence. Men came, spied on rumrunners for long, miserable hours in all weathers, told each other yarns of the dangers they faced, looked at the pittance in wages they were paid, and left in droves. But it was not necessary to leave the prohibition service to make money; it was possible to work for both sides at the same time— provided you didn't get caught! And many did get caught. The eleven year total of dismissals for accepting bribes, extortion, theft, forgery, violation of the Prohibition Act, falsification of records, conspiracy and perjury was sixteen hundred agents. The fact that one in twelve of all the agents hired was dismissed for wrongdoing gave a senator the opportunity to point out a precedent: of the twelve disciples of Jesus Christ, one went wrong. The ratio of good to bad in the Prohibition Bureau was no different.

Critics claimed that the sins of the agents, being no more than a reflection of the corruption of their leaders, were to be expected. The first prohibition director lasted a year and a half before giving up. His successor, claimed to be a man of "amazing genius and energy in organization" by his sponsoring congressman, fell short of his billing. His main talent seemed to be that of selling the message that bootlegging was on its last legs, when, in fact, it was thriving—and on his stimulation of departmental graft and corruption through the appointment of political friends. A third director, a retired general, was brought in to clean up the mess, and failed. His suggestion—made to a committee loaded with "dry" senators—that his task would be simplified if light wines and beer could be openly sold, brought about his speedy resignation. And when his clean-up attempts ended so abruptly, it was estimated that three out of four Prohibition Bureau officers were still "ward heelers and sycophants named by politicians."

If things were bad at the top of the Prohibition Bureau, there was not much chance of them being better at the middle levels of supervision. Parsimony and political influence still reigned. On the west coast, for example, Washington, Oregon and Alaska were part of the same huge prohibition district. But tremendous as it was in size, its budget was minute. In 1929, almost a decade into the fight to keep prohibition intact, it was reported that the district had only $34,000 to cover a sixteen-month period. By patronage, Roy C. Lyle of Seattle, sometime librarian and real-estate salesman, became prohibition administrator at a salary which would never rise above $6,000. During the ten years that he kept the job, Lyle's public image varied within a range bounded by pathetic at one end of the scale and comical at the other end. When asked what he intended to do about the new threat of smuggling by air, Lyle answered seriously that he was working on a lecture on the subject which he would give at a future convention of sheriffs. The answer was as good a measure as any of his lack of energy, forcefulness and imagination.

Lyle's chief assistant and legal adviser, William Whitney, led

Roy C. Lyle, given the impossible task of keeping the Northwest dry. *(photo courtesy of the Seattle Museum of History and Industry* [Seattle Post-Intelligencer *Collection]*)

the agents, and at an annual salary of around $5,000 was somewhat less affluent than his leader. But he was a much different man. Forthright and direct, Whitney had a talent for police work and a degree of ruthlessness in its application that lost him many friends. Raging mad at having their cars and homes searched for illicit booze by Whitney's overenthusiastic agents, many respectable Seattle residents wished to see him go. He stayed. Prohibition Bureau appointments were not made by democratic means; firings were no different.

The Prohibition Bureau in Washington State got off to a bad start. The Canadian border was impossible to patrol without a huge force of men. Vancouver Island looked south across the narrow Strait of Juan de Fuca to the scarcely populated shoreline of the Olympic Peninsula. The island-dotted expanse of the Strait of Georgia provided stepping stones where it was possible to pass from the Canadian Gulf Islands to the San Juans almost without being aware of the transition. And, to make things worse for those supposed to keep American lips unsullied by intoxicating drink, the long finger of Puget Sound poked its way down to the major liquor markets of Seattle and Tacoma. A rumrunner set to design a smuggler's paradise could not have improved on what nature had created. Nowhere on earth were rumrunning rewards so great; nowhere the risks so small. When Lyle's lack of effective power was recognized, a hundred rumrunners attended a convention in a Seattle hotel. Under *Robert's Rules of Order*, they adopted a resolution condemning narcotics smuggling, setting "fair" prices for bootlegged liquor, and establishing a code of "ethics" in order "to keep liquor runners within the limits of approved business methods." There could have been no more fitting illustration of the general weakness of the prohibition service and the contempt in which it was held.

The Prohibition Bureau and the United States Coast Guard were reducing the flow of illicit liquor entering the United States by hardly a trickle. And police forces and border patrols were doing no better. Common sense suggested that a combined force would increase overall effectiveness; the reality was that the distinct strands of enforcement, far from combining, spent more time on jurisdictional arguments and deliberate acts of non-cooperation than in attacking the major problem. The border patrols of the Bureau of Immigration, with their fixed aim of keeping the boundaries of the United States secure, were keen enough to stop smuggling carried out by aliens, but less concerned as to what citizens with a perfect right to be in the country were doing. Police forces of all sizes had dealt with prohibition for years before the passage of the Volstead Act made the creation of a Federal Prohibition Bureau necessary. They continued to be involved, but without extending much in the way of a hearty welcome to the upstart prohibition agents. In Seattle, where the local force arrested three federal prohibition agents for involvement in bootlegging, relations between the two organizations were particularly strained. But if the police mistrusted the prohibition agents, the agents mistrusted the police. And with reason. The jesting comment that Roy Olmstead commanded more police officers as a rumrunner than he had ever commanded as a police officer had a serious side. In acknowledging that there was police corruption, the chief of the Seattle Police Department pointed out that the dry law had opened up opportunities for graft in law enforcement that had never before existed. He was amazed that more police officers hadn't joined the other side than actually seemed to be the case.

On the other side of the border, there was a Canadian force set up to keep an eye on rumrunners and their suppliers, which was based on the government's interest in taxation. Was it a real threat? That depended as much on the rumrunning fraternity as it did on the customs authorities. If the $20-a-case export duty on liquor destined for the United States had been paid, there was no problem; if the tax had not been paid, there was a problem. $20-a-case duty to companies handling thousands of cases meant a heavy cash outlay with no resulting profit. Tax evasion was worthwhile— and easy. A simple declaration that the liquor was destined for anywhere in the world but the United States was all that was required. It was very difficult for the Canadian government to prove that the liquor had not been delivered to the declared destination. Like the United States Coast Guard, the Canadian customs force sent to sea to trap tax dodgers had its successes, but it, too, was far too small to make an appreciable dent in the problem.

Rumrunning paid well. The risks were small and rewards high. The opposing forces were weak, often corrupt, and more likely to work at cross purposes than to cooperate. Americans had created a monster they could never hope to overcome. Prohibition, as an act, was the law; prohibition, in fact, was a myth.

Capone's Chicago was a tough place. The evasion of the prohibition laws, a tough business. Profits derived from illicit booze financed the birth of organized-crime empires that still exist. But it is a combination of the situation and the people involved that decides how things will go. The west coast of North America had the same situation, but the people involved were not Capones. The story of west coast rumrunning has a unique feel created by a blend of past smuggling experiences, opportunity, the lie of the land, and a liberal dash of Pacific sea salt.

3
THE TERRIBLE TRIO

Never mind that his prisoners were known to be slippery customers, Jack Donnelly, assistant United States deputy marshal, felt
no unease when told to escort Ariel and Milo Eggers from their
holding cells to Commissioner Krull's office on the floor below.
The deputy marshal was in a federal building in the middle of
San Francisco, he was armed, it was broad daylight, and there was
a constant stream of people passing through the halls. In addition, away from their usual swashbuckling haunts and activities,
the Eggers brothers seemed mild and unthreatening. It was a
routine escort, no more.

The three men left the cell area and passed through a swing
door into a stairwell. Part way down the stairs, Milo Eggers stopped
and felt in his pocket. Donnelly tensed, and then just as quickly
relaxed. The cigarette packet in his prisoner's hand was harmless
enough. Eggers extracted a cigarette and placed it in his mouth.
Then he carefully closed the packet and returned it to his
pocket. Next there was a fumble for a packet of matches. The guard
and his prisoners had come to a stop. Milo Eggers struck a match,
lit the cigarette, inhaled deeply, and noisily exhaled. The puff of
smoke wreathing towards his face was the last thing Jack Donnelly
saw distinctly for a long time.

The leisurely act with the cigarette, designed to occupy

Donnelly's attention, worked brilliantly. Afterwards, the guard had a vague recollection of a group of men climbing the stairs towards where he and his prisoners were stopped. There were three men, he thought. He had not paid enough attention to them to be able to give any useful description of their appearances. When about to pass, one of the men had raised a large syringe, aimed its nozzle at the deputy marshal, and squeezed the ball. Instantly, a stream of ammonia hit Donnelly in the face and eyes. Blinded and in agony from facial burns, he staggered and started to drop to the floor. As he fell, one of the intruders fired at him with a revolver. The bullet missed the falling Donnelly and hit Ariel Eggers, who had been standing behind him. The men then grabbed Milo Eggers by the arms and hustled him towards the building exit. Clinging to the handrail for guidance, Jack Donnelly tried to make his way to the floor below, shouting for help as he went. Behind Donnelly, Ariel Eggers, hands clutched to a hole in his chest, weaved uncertainly. By the time help arrived he was dead.

Milo Eggers and his rescuers were soon gone. As they ran through the front door of the building, an open car moved quickly to the curb. They flung themselves on board and the car sped off. To discourage pursuit, one of the rescuers rode on the running board, waving his drawn revolver, gangland style. The car's registration number, CAL 116-029, was easily traced. But that was no help. Its owner had rented out the car earlier in the day. The names and addresses of the renters were, as might have been expected, false.

The reason for the Eggers' trip to Commissioner Krull's office was one that would have brought them no joy. Wanted by Canada for acts of piracy associated with rumrunning in 1923 and 1924, the arrangements for their extradition were about to be finalized. Waiting in the commissioner's office were Mrs. Erna Brown, sister to the Eggers, and Mrs. Dorothy Eggers, wife of Milo. At the sound of the shot, they, along with many others, rushed to the scene of the commotion. They had more reason than most to be appalled by what they saw. Erna Brown flung herself on the body of her slain brother, weeping hysterically and calling his name. The rescuers had gained a man and lost a man. They had freed Milo Eggers and killed Ariel Eggers in the process. The police believed that the fatal bullet had been fired by the third brother, Theodore Eggers.

It was a desperate incident, one of many in the wild rumrunning career of the Eggers brothers. Countless men broke the laws designed to keep America dry, and yet did little harm. But that was not the Eggers' way; naked greed caused them to behave in ways far beyond civilized limits.

Canadian officials waiting to escort the Eggers to Canada showed no surprise at the bizarre turn of events. For weeks they had been hearing stories that a jailbreak was in the offing. And, having themselves lost Ted (Theodore) Eggers on a previous occasion, they had reason to respect the Eggers' evasive capabilities.

When the body of Ariel Eggers had been removed, Dorothy Eggers and Erna Brown were placed under arrest and charged with conspiracy to murder Jack Donnelly. It was the opinion of Commissioner Krull that the women, seated in his office when the rescue attempt was made, were expecting something to happen. At the sound of the shot, Mrs. Brown had thrown her hands over her head and screamed, "My God!" as though recognizing that a planned event had gone awry. But that was only Krull's opinion; he had no proof. The women, penned in separate cells, were questioned at length but to no useful purpose. Whatever they knew was not for sharing with the questioning officers. The Eggers brothers had vanished. Milo, unwilling guest of the federal authorities for several months, was obviously wanted back again. Brother Ted, tagged as the rescuer of Milo, was wanted for the attempted murder of Donnelly and charges relating to the jailbreak. Police activity was intense. The police department knew the area of the city in which the fugitives were to be found, and arrests could be expected at any time—or so police spokesmen said. Sudden raids were made to no avail. The police claims were mere puffery; hot air to boost sagging morale in a time of failure. And, to make their discomfiture worse, it was being suggested that a plot was being hatched to free Dorothy Eggers and Erna Brown.

The Eggers clan was a painful problem for the various police forces of the west coast. For years its members had avoided capture; when captured, they seemed impossible to hold; and now, having escaped, they could not be found. But one person thought that the fugitive brothers were to be pitied rather than blamed. Their father, a wholesale fish merchant in the Puget Sound area, claimed that the apparent rescue attempt, far from being a plot designed by friends to liberate his sons, had been devised by their enemies to destroy them. Did not the death of his son, Ariel, bear witness to the truth of his words? And now Milo was missing, and probably in the hands of those who wished him harm. And the police were doing nothing about it, he complained.

From small beginnings, the Eggers brothers had worked hard to establish their notoriety. At first rumrunning had been easy and profitable. It could hardly have been otherwise when a case of liquor costing $25 in British Columbia could be sold for ten times that price in Seattle or Tacoma. The Eggers brothers, long in daring and short in respect for the law, made money fast and spent it just as fast. Life was good. But then, to their dismay, what had been easy became disturbingly difficult. And they knew why. Roy Olmstead was the root cause. A sound business organizer, he used bulk buying to slash his prices. Customers, naturally, flocked to him. And the nearer he edged to a monopoly of the liquor trade in the Puget Sound area, the more difficult it became for smaller, less efficient rumrunners to prosper.

On the verge of being squeezed out entirely, the Eggers supplied their own unique solution to the problem. Building the *M-197*, a sleek motorboat powered by a two hundred-horsepower engine, they set out to hijack the cargoes of other liquor traders. Stolen liquor was cheaper than bought liquor; that meant that they in turn would be able to sell at low prices and make money at the same time. Now Olmstead could have a taste of competition.

In the spring of 1923, Captain Tom Avery, skipper of the *Pauline*, became the Eggers' first victim. Lying off one of the Canadian Gulf Islands, the captain, alone in his boat, saw a fast speedboat approaching. That was a relief. His holds were packed with liquor from an offshore supply ship, and the waiting was always the hardest part of any smuggling operation. The speedboat would run the cargo across the line—that was the dangerous part—and he would take his money and head home. His relief was short-lived. It was the wrong speedboat. As he stood helpless, the *M-197* drew alongside and made fast to his vessel. And all the while her crew members brandished guns to discourage the merest thought of brave deeds. The 128 cases of liquor packed in the *Pauline*'s holds were rapidly loaded onto the *M-197*. And when all was safely stowed, she sped away with a roar of powerful engines. Hijacking was so easy. Jack Kearns and Billy

Burke, Seattle dealers in illicit spirits, would wait a long time for the load they had ordered from the Great Western Wine Company.

Rumrunner Johnny Schnarr suggested the means by which the Eggers got their information about rum cargoes. He also suggested the means by which they might be frightened off. Lazing on Discovery Island while waiting for a load of liquor, Schnarr took the time to watch two men who had arrived in a powerful, black-hulled boat. Imaginatively or not, he described them as rough looking characters, "hawk-faced, raw-boned." They were interested in the price of liquor and when supplies were due to arrive, but not interested enough to buy what was already available on the island, it seemed. Where then did their interest lie? In gathering information, thought Schnarr. To amuse themselves, the strangers tossed bottles into the sea and shot at them. After Johnny Schnarr's boat was loaded, he set out to make a delivery on the Washington shore. The black-hulled boat left with him. At D'Arcy Island, Schnarr ran up the eastern shore while the black speedboat ran up the western side. When the end of the island was reached, there was no sign of the black boat.

Schnarr was also a destroyer of bottles. In the presence of the strangers, he had joined in their activity and smashed three bottles with only three shots. The point had been made that he was armed and a good shot. That, he believed, was why the strangers had decided to leave him alone. He later learned that the black-hulled speedboat was owned by the Eggers brothers. The point of Schnarr's story was clear: if hijackers were armed, it made sense for their potential victims to be armed. A sensible conclusion, but one that must inevitably lead to an escalation of violence.

Perhaps Captain Emery, another Canadian supply-boat skipper, had listened and learned. When the *M-197* slid alongside the *Emma*, he stepped on deck with an automatic pistol in each hand. The Eggers pointed out the rough weather, their open boat, and their own miserable condition. They had called only to get warm and beg a cup of coffee. Or so they claimed. When their clothes were dry, they would move on, they said. Instead, they stayed the night and slept. Captain Emery stayed awake and kept his guns handy. In the morning, the brothers left with expressions of gratitude for the kindness of Emery. Schnarr's belief was confirmed. Guns were as useful for defending liquor cargoes as for hijacking them.

But the message of the guns had not reached all those in the rum trade. By D'Arcy Island the Eggers came across the *Erskine*. Her skipper, friendly, trusting and unarmed, invited them on board for coffee. It was an invitation too good to be refused. They accepted, climbed aboard, pulled guns and took charge. The *Erskine* and her cargo were taken across the Strait of Juan de Fuca. Half the cargo was hidden near Dungeness, on the American shore. The other half was loaded into the *M-197* and taken down to Seattle for immediate sale. This latest hijacking was a direct blow at the king of the rumrunners; the *Erskine*'s liquor cargo had been intended for delivery to Roy Olmstead.

Perhaps because of the true ownership of the *Erskine*'s cargo, it proved difficult to sell. Someone learned of the cargo and tried to blackmail the Eggers brothers. They owed him money, and he was prepared to make a deal. The debt could be paid off in liquor—at $50 a case. The price offered was ludicrous. Of course, it didn't have to be accepted. But then Olmstead would be told where to find his lost cargo. The threat made no difference; the brothers were not dealing at that price. Olmstead was told and a trap was set. One of his agents would lure the Eggers to a certain place, using as bait the possibility that he would buy the liquor. It was a double-dealing world. The Eggers found out about the trap and, on the day before they were due to be set up, barged into the hotel room of Olmstead's agent.

The room Prosper Grigniac had taken was on the sixth floor of the Commodore Hotel. Within minutes of the entry of Ariel and Ted Eggers, and after a brief shouting match, Grigniac had retreated before a jabbing revolver barrel until he had his back to the window. The window was open. Threatening Grigniac with a long drop, Ted Eggers took him by the throat and forced him backwards over the window sill. The sidewalk was a long way below. Grigniac, the sill under his bent knees, his feet off the floor, and only Ted Eggers's grip on his throat preventing him from falling, was sure that his last moment on earth was near. Eggers started to relax his grip. Grigniac's legs started to slither over the sill. He was beginning the promised long drop. Then he stopped with a jerk. Ariel Eggers, standing by, had clamped his legs on Grigniac's feet at the very last moment. He was jerked back into the room and started talking to save his neck. It would not do them any good to kill him, he said. That would make his friends all the more determined to get them. It didn't matter what he said, time was what he most needed. He sidled in the direction of the door as he spoke. Outside, elevator doors were opening. Grigniac wrenched the door open, leapt for the elevator, and in an instant the doors clanged shut and he was on his way down. At basement level, he dashed from the elevator and ran along the grimy corridor looking for a way of escape. In the boiler-room he saw a huge pile of sawdust reaching up the wall towards a small window. He climbed desperately, his feet sinking and slipping in the sawdust, until the window was within reach. He fumbled with the catch, pushed the window outward, squeezed his body through the narrow space, and tumbled into the alley running alongside the hotel. Picking himself up, he ran. Anywhere was better then the immediate vicinity of the Commodore Hotel and the Eggers brothers.

What the Eggers brothers were doing had an ancient name—piracy. In the tradition of those who had once flown the Jolly Roger, they were stealing ship's cargoes by force. True enough, the cargoes had changed from Spaniard's gold to gunny-sacked liquor, but that also led to gold of a sort. Their dress was different too, and cutlasses had been replaced by revolvers, but the process was much the same. The overall shape of the liquor supply system set their area of operations and picked their victims. Attacking large liquor supply ships in international waters was impossible; intercepting fast speedboats, like their own, as they ran at full throttle for American shores, impractical. The weak link in the supply chain occurred among the Canadian Gulf Islands, where small boats met fast American speedboats and handed over liquor cargoes picked up from the mother ships. The Canadian-registered boats, manned by Canadians sailing in Canadian waters, were slow and their crews easy to trap. It was an ideal situation for the Eggers brothers and one of great frustration for the Canadian government. Outraged by acts of piracy within sight of its shores, government agents swore to end the Eggers' depredations. But first they had to catch them.

Canadian threats of retribution had not the slightest effect on the Eggers. In August 1923 they found another victim. Adolf Ongstad and Jack Webster were sailing the liquor-ladened *Lillums* towards a rendezvous off North Pender Island when they spotted the *M-197* moving quietly along in the shadow of a nearby island.

Sensibly, they headed for the nearest shore. It seemed unlikely that a hijacking would be tried with the *Lillums* moored at the pier of a busy waterfront resort.

With his companion gone to arrange a new rendezvous with the captain of the boat they had failed to meet, Ongstad was left alone. As darkness fell, not completely certain that he was safe, he struggled to stay awake and alert. But there had to be a breaking point. Eventually, his head, too heavy for his shoulders, flopped forward. He jerked upright and fought to stay awake. His weary eyes ached. His eyelids drooped and then he slept. Shortly afterwards, the Eggers came quietly alongside, guns drawn, and overpowered the sleeping Ongstad with no trouble. Then they towed the *Lillums* well away from the shore, took her cargo, and set Adolf Ongstad adrift with the ignition wires removed from his motor. Charles Foster, sitting on an Everett dock awaiting his cargo, had just lost 150 cases of liquor.

On the first Monday evening of March 1924, the American vessel *Kayak* had just moored off a Canadian island when a speedboat eased alongside. On her deck were four masked men, each with a rifle in hand. In minutes Troy Martin and Joe Edwards were trussed like oven-bound turkeys and in no better condition to help themselves. They protested that the *Kayak*'s holds were empty. And so they were. But the intruders seemed unconcerned by the fact.

After concealing the speedboat, the pirate crew lay in wait all Monday night. They were obviously not in a hurry. At midday on Tuesday they got the *Kayak* underway. To Troy Martin, still roped and fuming at his helplessness, their destination was soon clear. The course was right and the time was right. They were going to Peters Cove, an indentation on North Pender Island's shore, to keep his appointment with the liquor carrier *Hadsel*. It was no wonder that the empty holds had left them undisturbed.

The vessels met offshore. The crew of the *Hadsel* were cautious. And with reason. Adolf Ongstad, caught once before by hijackers, was on board. As the boats neared, one of the hijackers prodded Martin with a gun and got him on deck where he could be easily seen. The *Hadsel* crew knew Martin; their fears were allayed. The vessels closed. At a range of twenty feet, the *Kayak*'s captors loosed off a barrage of rifle fire. Ongstad escaped unhurt but his companion was hit. Later, the wounded man told how he had cursed the hijackers as he lay on the deck. Were they crazy? he wanted to know. Were they trying to kill him? The reply from one of the masked bandits was hardly apologetic: "It's too bad we didn't kill you."

Eventually, the four captives were put on the *Kayak* and set adrift. They watched impotently as the hijackers sailed the *Hadsel* away, liquor cargo and all. It would take time for word to get through to Roy Olmstead that 226 cases of already paid for liquor, valued at about $10,000, had gone astray.

Who had carried out the hijacking? More than the police wanted to know. Splashy newspaper headlines made great play of the fact—if it was a fact—that "legitimate" rumrunners were helping the police to run down the pirates. According to a veteran of the smuggling game, three of the men on the speedboat were brothers. As this veteran was said to be one of the leading rumrunners on Puget Sound, it was highly likely that he was Roy Olmstead. Olmstead had good reason to want the hijackers caught. Over the past year or so, this same group of hijackers had made off with more the $170,000 worth of booze, and he had paid for a considerable portion of it.

The pressure on the Eggers brothers became too great for them to bear. They cut their losses and ran for California. But first the *M-197* was sold to three Seattle men. She brought them no luck. Her first load was hijacked! The second cargo was jettisoned to escape capture by the coast guard. And during a third rumrunning attempt, she limped into Roche Harbor, on the San Juan Islands, with a crippled engine. Roy Olmstead had the reputation of being opposed to violence. Perhaps that was violence towards people and not things. Or possibly some of his men were inclined to take things into their own hands; a group of them, finding the disabled *M-197*, towed her out to deep water, punched holes in her hull, and left her to sink. If the Eggers brothers could not be caught, then their old boat must pay for their sins. There was a certain rough justice in the act.

The brothers' activities in and around San Francisco were not blessed with success. On November 9, 1924, Ariel and Milo were arrested and it was this event that led to the freeing of Milo and the death of Ariel. Within weeks it was reported that another brother had also died violently.

Pillar Point was the last place the inhabitants of nearby Half-moon Bay would have chosen to visit on a dark night. It was there that liquor supplies were landed from Rum Row and there that hijackers tried to wrest newly landed liquor cargoes from their rightful owners. That being so, no one was greatly surprised when a fisherman reported seeing a body washing slackly in the breaking waves off the point.

A sheriff's posse recovered the body. This had been no accidental death. The body, brutally mutilated, was covered in deep gashes. Where the hands and feet had been, there were now only ghastly stumps. The man appeared to have been between 35 and 40 years of age, to have been 5 feet 11 inches tall, and to have weighed about 190 pounds. There was not much available to help in establishing identity, but when the investigation was over the police had come to the conclusion that the remains were those of Milo Eggers. He had lived by hijacking and, it was assumed, he had died at the hands of hijackers. It was a wishful kind of identification and quite wrong.

Six months after the presumed demise of Milo, Theodore Eggers was arrested in Seattle and sent to Canada for trial on hijacking charges. His capture had been difficult and his conviction was impossible. Witnesses from the liquor supply boats concerned failed to identify him as one of the men who had stolen their liquor cargoes. "Terror of the Eggers and their gang is thought to have had some influence on these witnesses," a local newspaper dryly reported.

If the Canadians could not nail Ted Eggers, the United States had unfinished business to conclude. Passed back across the border, he was sentenced to six months in prison for assisting Milo to escape. It wasn't much, but it was more than had ever been pinned on him before.

It was two years later that the law caught up with the very much alive Milo Eggers. Taken in Tacoma, he was his usual cocky self. The Canadian authorities would have no success in extraditing him, he said. His captors, expecting an effort by his friends to free him, thought he might be right. But the extradition proceedings moved quickly and an extradition order was signed. It was not intended that there should be any delay in carrying it out. Inspector Forbes Cruickshank of the British Columbia provincial police moved quickly to get Eggers into Canadian jurisdiction. With a United States marshal and a shotgun squad, he went to the jail to pick up Milo. But Eggers refused to budge from his cell. Making the best of what was available, he picked up a heavy pot and threatened, "Come in and I'll knock your heads off." The shot guns were raised and aimed at his heart. It was no contest. Cursing bitterly, he shambled from the cell. The possibility of escape still pressed, and no chances were being taken. The coast guard vessel *Arcata* was assigned the task of getting Milo Eggers to British Columbia. An entire ship for one man!

In Victoria a few weeks later, Magistrate Jay had just ordered that Milo Eggers should be remanded for trial at the fall assizes and was staring with astonishment at the scene around the prisoner's dock. Eggers, on hearing the decision, had burst into tears, and surging forward were the members of his family bent on offering their comfort. His elderly mother got there first, threw her arms around him and smothered him with kisses, all the while brushing away his tears with her gloved hands. His wife, next in line, sobbed and kissed him time and time again. His sister embraced the weeping man, and finally his father, a undemonstrative person by family comparison, shook his son's hand firmly. It was a remarkable sight: Milo Eggers, one of the terrible trio that had terrorized the rumrunning fraternity, weeping like a child. The magistrate, unable to tolerate such unseemly behavior in his court, waved into action police officers who grasped Milo Eggers by the arms and hustled him out of the courtroom.

The tears were probably caused by rage. Eggers had confidently expected acquittal. Now this! He had a rock-solid alibi. His father swore that Milo was in Seattle, under his supervision during the entire spring of 1924, and had certainly not left the city during the first five days of March. Conveniently, the hijacking had occurred on March 3. Dorothy Eggers, Milo's wife, backed her father-in-law's story to the hilt, and Milo's mother corroborated her daughter-in-law's testimony. And she was testy about it. During cross-examination by the prosecution, she frostily demanded, "Why do you ask such foolish questions? I have already answered that." The prosecutor's comment that her answer had been given to the defense counsel, not to him, drew a sharp retort. "Well, if you heard me say it to him, what's the difference?" Backing off seemed not to be a family trait. Clearly, the family was solidly behind Milo, and he had good friends in court to give added support. Chris Olsen, a Seattle fish broker, told of

Eggers packing cod for him during the first four days of March. He had paid him $28 for his work. Wages of $7 a day for a man accused of having stolen a liquor cargo worth $10,000! Perhaps some of the fish packing money had been used to pay for admission to a prize fight in Tacoma. According to Harold MacMillan, Milo and he had enjoyed the bout together during the evening of Monday, March 3. The prosecution was in trouble. With such an alibi, how could it be proven that Milo Eggers was one of the masked men that had taken the *Kayak* and used her as a decoy to capture the *Hadsel* and her cargo? The crew of the *Hadsel* could not, or would not, identify Eggers. They could not see through masks. But one man had seen. One of the men had briefly pulled aside his mask, and Troy Martin, skipper of the *Kayak*, had recognized him as Milo Eggers. Had he been there as Martin had said, or had he not? The magistrate dithered briefly. As he saw it, the presence of Milo Eggers at the hijacking of the *Hadsel* had not been clearly established. Eggers and his supporters began to smile. On the other hand, the magistrate went on, there had been some evidence of identification at the crime scene. The smiles faded. On balance, there was reason enough to send the accused to trial. That was when the unexpected flood of tears had flowed.

October rolled around, bringing with it the fall assizes. This time the trial would end in sentencing or acquittal. Milo Eggers had spent several months in Oakalla Prison and he was pale and drawn, but defiant. Asked to plead guilty or not, he refused to do either. He believed that he had been railroaded and should have been released after the initial hearing. On his behalf, his counsel contended that the case was not properly before the court and to plead would be an admission that it was. To the layman that meant nothing. But laymen were not involved in the argument. In private, judge, prosecutor and defense counsel argued. After forty-five minutes they returned. The judge offered Eggers the chance to have the status of the case placed before a jury. Eggers, no doubt seeing another long wait in jail, refused the offer. But he still would not plead. The judge entered a plea of not guilty on his behalf, and the case began in earnest.

The prosecution's case still rested tenuously on the identification of Milo Eggers by Troy Martin. And that was based on no more than a glimpse when an obscuring face-mask had been pulled down. The *Kayak*'s crew had been reluctant to appear at the preliminary hearing and the intervening months had not changed their distaste for testifying against one of the Eggers trio. Perhaps they had been provided with good reason to be reluctant. When the trial opened, Joe Edwards was missing. He was, he claimed, very sick and intended to stay at home in Seattle until cured of whatever ailed him. But Troy Martin, the sole identifier of Milo Eggers, was there. He had not changed much, but his evidence certainly had.

Crown Prosecutor Johnson's opening question to Troy Martin was confident enough. "Are you able to identify the man who took his mask off that night on the launch *Kayak*?"

The unexpectedly hesitant reply had a discouraging ring. "Well, yes."

Johnson, slightly puzzled, pressed on. "Is that man in the courtroom here today?"

"I don't know," the witness replied.

"Look around the courtroom, Mr. Martin, and see if you can see him."

Martin's eyes stopped on Milo Eggers. "That man in the prisoner's dock is the one I identified in Tacoma," he said.

The defense counsel objected to the answer. The witness must answer the question; he had not been asked whom he had identified in Tacoma.

The judge put the original question to the witness. "Is the man you saw on the *Kayak* in this courtroom?"

"Well, I couldn't say definitely," answered Martin.

Prosecutor Johnson persisted. "Does the man in the dock in any way resemble the man you saw on the *Kayak*?"

Martin took his time. He looked over Eggers critically and then answered. "Well, he was a lightly complected man."

"And what about his build?"

"He was a heavier man than the accused."

"And as to his height?"

"The man here is a little shorter."

Archie Johnson was nearing the end of his patience. His frustration showed in his tone. "Can you give any further description of the man who removed his mask?"

"No."

Milo Eggers' alibi had been disbelieved at the preliminary hearing. Now it would be more difficult to ignore. The judge drew the attention of the jury to the fundamental principle of justice: innocence is presumed until the fact of guilt is proven beyond reasonable doubt. The jury left the courtroom to consider a verdict. Twenty-five minutes later they were back to say that Milo Eggers was not guilty of robbery with violence in the case of the *Hadsel* hijacking.

Twisting the knife in the wound, Eggers' counsel reminded the judge that an acquittal carried an obligation to pay the costs of the defendant. His lordship seemed not in the best of tempers. He snapped, "That can come up for argument later."

There were many in British Columbia who still believed Milo Eggers to be as guilty as sin. His witnesses—family and friends—had lied on his behalf. Tens of thousands of dollars had been spent on bringing Milo Eggers to trial, and it had been wasted. There was, perhaps, a small consolation to be found. Since being taken in Tacoma, by police officers armed with tear gas bombs, he had been kept in prison. For the skeptical, that was some small measure of justice. Of events immediately following the verdict a reporter wrote, somewhat snarkily, "immigration officers were ordered to escort him to the border and wash their hands of him." It was not quite that way. He left Victoria for Seattle by ferry, in the normal way. If Canadian reporters had the last word on Milo Eggers as he left Victoria, then American reporters had the first word as he landed in Seattle. In the first place, they had trouble recognizing him. He had changed. They wrote, imaginatively perhaps, of an emaciated face marked by a prison pallor. To them, he seemed a beaten man as he hurried, cap pulled low over his eyes and overcoat collar turned up, from the *Emma Alexander* and fled along the passageway leading down to the street level. He had nothing to say.

One thing was certain: they had counted him out too soon. Four days after Milo Eggers had arrived home, a patrolling police officer noticed a car parked outside a theater in the early morning hours. Two women were sitting in the car—uneasily, it seemed to the officer. He questioned them and was told that their husbands had gone off looking for moonshine. The officer, still suspicious, moved off a little way. Immediately, one of the women blasted the car horn in what sounded very much like a pre-arranged signal. Men ran from the direction of the theater, bundled into the car, and started to drive off with no time wasted.

The officer ran towards the car, but was too late to intercept it. Where the car had stood, a revolver and a flashlight lay on the ground. His suspicions had been well founded. Two shots fired after the fast-retreating car had no effect.

The hunt was on. Within two days six people were arrested "in connection with the attempted robbery of the Baghdad Theater." The arrests took place in an apartment in which there were bags already packed for flight. The apartment was that of Dorothy and Milo Eggers. They were two of the six arrested. From being in the custody of the British Columbia police to being in the custody of the Seattle police had taken not much more than a week.

Clearly, the Eggers brothers were a spent force as far as hijacking went. Their importance lay in that they had introduced a viciousness into rumrunning that had not been there at its inception. Unfortunately, others would follow their path, and murder would result.

4
FULL FATHOMS FIVE

It was September, and the early morning air was cool. Pete Marinoff shivered slightly as he looked over the misty waters of Puget Sound. One of his speedboats was overdue, and he feared trouble. But perhaps he was worrying unduly, for soon he heard throttled-back speedboat engines. It sounded like his boat. And it was. As he watched, the rumrunning craft appeared from behind a small point of land. Close to the dock, the helmsman cut the engines, and the only sound was that of burbling water as the flared bow gently parted the waters. Marinoff caught the thrown mooring rope, looped it around a bollard, and made fast. A truck moved forward. Liquor cargoes had to be unloaded fast and rushed to secure hiding places.

It occurred to Marinoff that the boat was riding higher in the water than usual. It occurred to Herbert Hodge that his employer would not much relish what he was about to hear. Things had been going well, but now there was a real problem.

When Hodge stepped ashore, he walked towards Pete Marinoff shaking his head. "They weren't there," he said.

"They weren't there?" The message seemed not to register with Pete Marinoff. "What do you mean, they weren't there?"

"They just weren't there. Not a sign of them. Gone."

Marinoff's speedboat had gone out empty and had returned

The ill-fated *Beryl G. (photo courtesy of the Vancouver Maritime Museum)*

empty. It was as simple as that. He waved the waiting truck away.

A few days ago one third of the *Beryl G*'s cargo of whisky had been picked up by Hodge and delivered to the very dock on which they stood. And now the wooden freighter had vanished with the remaining 240 cases of whisky still in her hold. That lot had cost him over $6,000, and would have sold for ten times as much.

Marinoff next heard of the *Beryl G* at the same time as all the other newspaper readers around Puget Sound. A report from the San Juan Islands told of her drifting up to the rocks at the foot of the Turn Point light on Stuart Island, crewless and with empty holds. The theory that she had broken away in the storm that had lashed the Strait of Georgia the night before, leaving her crew stranded on some uninhabited island, was quickly abandoned. Why would men leave a boat with her hatch covers off and land on such an island? What purpose could they have had for such a visit?

And then there was the blood.

Chris Waters, keeper of the light, with the aid of Eric Erickson, the local postmaster, had snagged the drifting boat and towed it to shore. They had been the first to enter the *Beryl G*'s cabin. It seemed that a fight had occurred. Blankets had been torn from the bunks and lay in crumpled heaps. The cabin deck was ankle deep in litter. Among the unwashed plates on the cabin table rested a gold-braided seaman's cap. The cap contained a mess of congealed blood. Aghast, Waters and Erickson had jostled each other to be first up the companionway and back into the sweet, fresh air. But escaping the blood was not easy. There were red smears on the deck, on the bulwarks, and on a heap of wet clothing lying near the bow. The salvagers of the *Beryl G* called the police; this was not a matter for a lighthouse keeper and a rural postmaster.

American investigators swiftly got rid of the problem. The *Beryl G* was of Canadian registry, and the set of the currents causing her to arrive at the foot of the Turn Point light suggested that whatever had happened on board had happened in Canadian waters. The boat was towed away from Friday Harbor by the British Columbia provincial police, depriving visitors to the local county fair of an unexpected, though grisly, attraction.

The Canadian police now held a vessel that had officially cleared Victoria for Nitinat, far up the west coast of Vancouver Island, with empty holds. Why then should the holds not be empty? But what was the *Beryl G* doing on the eastern side of Vancouver Island at no great distance from her starting point days after her departure? And what of the blood? A Victoria hospital pathologist confirmed that it was human blood. But who had bled? And why? There was no trace of Captain Gillis and his son: not on the vessel; not on any of the Gulf Islands that had been searched; and not under the surrounding waters, so far as the results of patient dragging had revealed.

Naturally, there was dockside gossip. Rumrunners were whispering behind the backs of their hands that hijackers had taken a cargo of liquor from the *Beryl G* and had murdered Captain Gillis and his son to cover their tracks. Nitinat! The west coast of Vancouver Island! Never. Gillis had been out to Rum Row to pick up 350 cases of liquor from the *Comet*. While lying by the supply ship's side, he had repaired his balky engine and had left for Sidney Island to meet his American contact when all seemed well. The details given were specific and numerous enough to make the truth of the whispered stories probable. And if everyone knew as much about the affairs of Captain Gillis as the gossips, arranging a hijacking would have been easy. But if the police believed that a hijacking had led to the killing of the Gillis father and son, they were trading in supposition. More than dockside gossip was needed. There were two bullet holes in the hull of the *Beryl G.* But who had fired the shots? Captain Gillis had a reputation for truculence, owned a gun, and would not hesitate to use it if pressed. Boarding his boat uninvited would have provided pressure enough. The holes in the hull could have been made by bullets from his gun. It was conceivable that Captain Gillis had killed someone and then disappeared.

Murders without bodies. Rumrunning without bottles. Here was a fine mystery!

Two things found on the *Beryl G* had promise as clues. One was the sailor's cap first seen by Erickson and Waters: white, where it wasn't bloodstained, and with a shiny black peak liberally decorated with gold trim. Neither Gillis had owned it. To whom, then, did it belong? Was it possible to trace the ownership of a seaman's cap that might have been bought in any seaport in the world? The second clue was a film with a single frame exposed, found in a cheap camera. The film, developed, provided a hazy photograph of the stern of a powerful motorboat, apparently pulling away from the *Beryl G*'s. Faint characters on the boat's transom showed her registration number to be *M-493*.

Inspector Forbes Cruickshank must have received the news of his assignment to the *Beryl G* case with no great joy. In his fifties, he was a large and comfortable man not far from a well-earned retirement. Age, it seemed, brought no relief. Poking around the sordid fringes of rumrunning for murderers—if murder had been done—promised to be an unpleasant task. Yet no better man could have been assigned. Cruickshank was intelligent, tenacious and tough. He was not a man to back away from problems. And one problem was of special concern; *M-493* was an American registration number. His investigation would have to begin in the United States.

Cruickshank had worked with American police forces many times in the past and had always been welcomed with open arms. But prohibition times were different. Many American police officers, tempted by money far beyond what they could honestly earn, were rumrunner's spies; men who might make his mission known and his survival unsure. No official contact could be made. He would have to operate as a private detective—and an unlicensed one at that. He would be an alien poking around among the citizens of a foreign country in the hope of finding the perpetrators of a crime he could not prove had been committed.

Seattle was Forbes Cruickshank's starting point. The city, standing with its feet in the waters of Puget Sound, was the focus of northwestern rumrunning. In the records of the locks leading into Union Bay were entries showing that the *M-493* often passed that way. Her owner was Pete Marinoff.

Inspector Cruickshank had heard of Marinoff. And not all that he had heard was bad. Marinoff, known as "Legitimate Pete," stuck to his trade and kept well away from the protection rackets, prostitution and gunplay that were the marks of eastern rumrunners. That was comforting to the man who must eventually interview Marinoff. But if Cruickshank thought that physical danger was unlikely in such an interview, he was well aware that being laughed at was a strong possibility. Why should a rum baron talk about his business to him?

When Cruickshank and Marinoff met, the rumrunner was cautious. He agreed that he had heard of the *Beryl G*. But then, so had tens of thousands of others; the story of her hijacking had been in all the local papers. Why, he wanted to know, had Cruickshank come to him? The inspector passed over the photograph of the *M-493* found on the *Beryl G*. Pete Marinoff shrugged. Somewhere, at sometime, his speedboat had passed the *Beryl G*— and many others like her, no doubt. That proved nothing. Forbes Cruickshank agreed.

Marinoff's mind raced. The loss of a liquor cargo at heavy cost still rankled. This alien policeman was no threat and might be of use. Cruickshank might just be the man to help him get revenge and prevent future losses. If murder had been committed on the *Beryl G* it would be a hanging matter. What a message a hanging would send to potential hijackers!

Marinoff talked. Yes, Gillis had been hauling a cargo for him on the *Beryl G*. There had been 350 cases of liquor on board; good stuff. Fortunately, he had been lucky enough to get some of those cases delivered to Tacoma. The men who had picked up the first load had gone back for a second, only to find that the *Beryl G* and her crew had disappeared. He knew no more than that. Cruickshank had made progress. The gossip of the Victoria waterfront about the *Beryl G*'s rumrunning activities had proven to be remarkably accurate. The hijacking theory was now tenable. But where did that lead? To another dead-end, as far as Forbes Cruickshank could tell.

Cruickshank had nowhere to go, and Marinoff had nothing more to tell. Perhaps "Legitimate Pete" was having second thoughts. Talking openly to a police officer was not what he did best. Yet the thought of ending hijackings still held an attraction. As they parted, he squeezed out a few more words. "Al Clausen might know something."

On the surface, Al Clausen was simply a garage owner. In fact, most of his money came from hiring out a powerful speed-boat, with his services as mechanic and operator included in the price. By hints of possible extradition to Canada to face serious charges if he didn't cooperate, the inspector got Clausen to talk of a late-September trip when cached liquor had been recovered from several Canadian island locations. Then, on Pender Island, the recovered bottles had been put in new sacks daubed with a large green C. The green paint had come from a local farmer. Later, some of the liquor had been taken to a dealer in Anacortes. When it came to naming the men who had hired his boat, Al Clausen became stubborn. If they heard that he had ratted on them he would be in serious trouble. But they were out of sight and Cruickshank, trouble of another kind, was within reach. He talked. Charlie Morris was there. "Si" Sowash, too—Harry was his real name. And—the final name seemed to stick in his throat—Owen Baker. "Cannonball" Baker. On the trip to Anacortes, Baker had told him that the liquor had been taken from "the old man and the boy."

Cruickshank prodded. "Which old man? Which boy?" Clausen assumed that Baker was speaking of Captain Gillis and his son. It was an assumption that any competent lawyer could have torn to ribbons in short order.

The matter of the bloodied seaman's cap was unresolved. Dozens of Seattle sales clerks had told Forbes Cruickshank that it was not possible to identify the purchaser of an ordinary seaman's cap, and then he found one who could and did. Harry Kerrigan flicked through a collection of sales slips until one caught his attention. A note, in his own handwriting, said that he had forgotten to charge for a set of brass buttons. Brass buttons and a seaman's cap, bought at the same time? Kerrigan's face lit up. "The rumrunner," he said, "I'll bet it was the rumrunner."

He remembered asking a customer if he wanted the cap of any particular shipping line. "Line, hell," had been the reply, "I'm running booze out of Canada. All I need is an official-looking cap so that I can talk myself out of trouble if I get picked up."

Cruickshank passed Harry Kerrigan a bundle of photographs secured by an elastic band. "Here. Have a look through these. Let me know if you recognize anyone."

Halfway through the bundle, Kerrigan paused. Cruickshank held his breath. Kerrigan said nothing and went on to the end of the bundle. There was a light in his eye. He started through the bundle again. When he came to the photograph that had caused him to pause on the first pass, he held it out to the inspector. "There he is. There's the rumrunner. But I can't tell you his name."

Inspector Cruickshank turned over the photograph that Harry Kerrigan had selected. Neatly lettered on the back was the name Owen Benjamin Baker. "Cannonball" Baker, the man who had boasted to Al Clausen about taking liquor from the old man and the boy.

A sack with a green, painted *C* turned up in Anacortes. The rum dealer who had supplied the sack and its spirituous contents to a local physician just happened to be in the local jail awaiting trial. In the interests of helping his own case he was willing to name his supplier—it was Owen Baker. Sergeant Bob Owens, mercifully released from the fruitless task of dragging the bottom of the Strait of Georgia, made good use of his contacts to gather snippets of information for Cruickshank. Anything was grist for his mill, providing it had happened close to September 16, 1924, the apparent date of the *Beryl G* hijacking. A boat-yard in Victoria had done modifications on the upper works of an old gas boat a day or so after that date. *Denman II* was her name. Odd thing, said the boatyard owner. There was no good reason for the changes. He had seen no sign of weakness or rot. Changed her appearance though, no better or worse—just different. Owned by a man called Stromkins. Polish, by the sound of him.

On Pender Island, Bob Owens found Clausen's farmer, the one who had provided green paint to mark the rebagged liquor. From photographs, the farmer identified Baker, Sowash and Clausen as the men involved. Al Clausen's story was holding up. Owens had included a photograph of Stromkins in his collection. Farmer Thorsten Paulson chuckled when he saw it. "Why, there's Paul. Paul

Paul Stromkins, chief prosecution witness at the *Beryl G* trial, with wife. (*photo courtesy the Seattle Museum of History and Industry* [Seattle Post-Intelligencer *Collection*])

Stromkins. I knew him in Manitoba before we moved west. See him sometimes when he is running beer to the States."

On Lopez Island, in the San Juans, Owens found that Paul Stromkins had called in for gas on the morning after the presumed hijacking. Why had he been caught short of gas on that day, part way between the American and Canadian shores? It would be worth having a talk with Paul Stromkins.

But Stromkins was elusive. And before he was found, Owens had a talk with a customs agent who knew Baker and Sowash. They had tried to pump him for information on rumrunning in the middle of a park in Victoria. The nervy pair had been introduced to him by a Vancouver Island resident—fellow by the name of Paul Stromkins.

The *Denman II* was often to be found at anchor just off the premises of the Victoria Yacht Club on Cadboro Bay. Club steward Robert Harrap knew the boat well. He also knew Paul Stromkins. He had last seen boat and man on his last late shift in September—must have been the fifteenth. A couple of men had come down to the dock and Stromkins had rowed them out to the *Denman II*. Soon after, she had sailed.

Then a tip from a taxi driver led Sergeant Owens to a house

on Balmoral Road in Victoria. There Mrs. Hazel Feasey told him that she had frequently entertained Paul Stromkins, Owen Baker, Charlie Morris and Harry Sowash when they were in town on business. What business was that? Mrs. Feasey shrugged and replied that they spent most of their time talking about rumrunning. He could draw whatever conclusion he liked from that.

Now it was imperative that Paul Stromkins be interrogated. He was eventually found and questioned, and it proved to be a great waste of time. He knew nothing; no one. He owned the *Denman II*, they suggested. No, he did not. They knew he did. No, he had sold it. Why had he gone to the trouble to have work done on the boat and then got rid of it? The changes had made it better, easier to sell. Anyway, it was none of their business. What did he know of the *Beryl G*? Nothing more than he had read in the newspapers. In his opinion, they would be better employed solving that mystery rather than harassing him. Did he know Owen Baker? No. Did he know Harry Sowash? No. A customs agent had seen him with them. Then the agent was lying. Did he know Charlie Morris? No. A steward at the yacht club had seen him row Baker and Morris out to the *Denman II*. He was lying. A woman on Lopez Island had supplied him with gas on September 16. She was lying. He had never been to Lopez Island in his life. Paulson, a friend of his from their days together in Manitoba, knew that he was a rumrunner—or was it just beer that he ran over the line? It was neither. And who was Paulson? Paul Stromkins insisted that he had never heard of him.

The man was in a highly nervous state. What would it take to break him? A plan was devised. Thorsten Paulson, brought from Pender Island for the occasion, was interviewed again. Why, he could not imagine. He had nothing new to say. The interview, dragged out in its early stages, ended abruptly when the officer in charge looked at his watch, thanked Paulson shortly and ushered him swiftly to the door. At the other side of the door another officer was urging Paul Stromkins forward with a firm hand in the small of his back. The door opened and Paulson stepped out. Stromkins stopped dead, recognition flooded his face, he smiled and said, "Hello, Paulson. What are you doing here?" Then he realized what he had done. But it was too late to take back the words.

Caught in a lie, Stromkins tipped over the edge. Now he could not get the words out fast enough to tell what he knew of the *Beryl G* and the murders of Captain Gillis and his son. He had been a minor player, he insisted. Morris, Sowash and Baker were the guilty ones. Confession was such a relief. He had been tortured by his secret knowledge, had wanted to tell but fear had held him back.

Extradition proceedings were started to get Owen Baker, Harry Sowash and Charlie Morris, all American citizens, sent to Canada for trial. Morris was easy to find. The other two had disappeared from their usual Seattle haunts.

Charlie Morris, a small-time crook who had done time for selling fake gold coins to gullible Seattle residents, was soon arrested. His jail experience had strengthened rather than reformed his tendency to take the easy, illegal way to riches. Prohibition days were ideal for such as he. Brash and not too bright, it had not occurred to him to get as far away from Seattle as possible when the *Beryl G* story broke. They would never get him, he boasted. It depended on who "they" were. The Seattle police found him easily enough, but that hardly counted. Getting him to trial in Canada was the problem. A successful Canadian bid for his extradition was only the beginning of a long road. The lawyer acting for Morris, set to go as far as the Supreme Court of the United States if necessary, warned of years of appeals.

Sowash and Baker, more intelligent than Morris and perhaps with more to fear, had disappeared from Seattle at the first sign of trouble. Wanted posters were sent out which gave the promise of a significant reward for their capture. Two minor players in crime had suddenly become major leaguers.

Harry Sowash was caught in a routine police net cast to rid New Orleans streets of undesirables and was released with apologies. The youngest son of a wealthy eastern family, he was mannerly, well educated and able to make a good impression when it suited his purpose—and the false identity documents he produced helped to divert suspicion. Almost too late, a police officer, musing over where he had seen that face before, remembered that it had been on a wanted poster. Sowash, prowling the docks for a boat leaving the United States, was arrested and turned over to the Canadian police. On the long journey to Vancouver's Oakalla Prison, he wrote a one-sided "confession." Led astray by Owen Baker, a former prison acquaintance, Sowash claimed to have played a minor role in the hijacking. It had all been Baker's idea and when things went wrong Baker had cold-bloodedly killed the *Beryl G*'s crew.

Owen Baker, under the alias of George Nolan, was picked up in New York City where he was working on a dredger. His attempt to avoid extradition by a long courtroom recital of how unfair Canadian juries were to American citizens failed to impress. His plea to have witnesses brought from Hawaii to New York to give him an alibi for the time of the *Beryl G* hijacking fell on deaf ears. He was resistant to the judge's advice to face up to the problem and go voluntarily to Canada to prove his innocence. But, finally, it was the judge's decision rather than his advice that brought the extradition hearing to a close. Like Sowash before him, "Cannonball" Baker journeyed under escort across the continent to hear Oakalla's iron gates clang behind him.

With the arrival of Baker, three of the four accused of complicity in the *Beryl G* affair were behind bars in Oakalla jail. Only Charlie Morris, still resisting extradition, was free. Paul Stromkins was the edgy one; to no one's surprise, local newspapers reported that he had attempted suicide. The prison warden poured scorn on the report. "Mr. Stromkins is contented and has expressed no worry except over his wife. We have told him that she is being cared for. He has asked to be allowed to work in the tailor's shop, and he is there now, busily sewing on buttons." In association with a case of bloody murder, the warden's words had a comic ring. And the jailhouse farce was not over. Harry Sowash tried to lower a magazine to Owen Baker in the cell immediately below, and failed. The string broke and the magazine fell to the ground where it was found by a prison guard. When the warden examined the magazine, tucked within its pages was a copy of Sowash's confession that had damned Baker, along with suggestions as to how all the accusations could be explained away. Why Harry Sowash had gone to all this trouble was never made clear. Possibly he feared retribution if a released Baker ever caught up with him in the future. Possibly he had genuine regrets. An attorney, putting a brave face on a bad situation, later suggested that Sowash was trying to provide his partner with loopholes out of sympathy for Baker's wife and son. What would become of them if Owen Baker was convicted?

In March 1925, a preliminary hearing of the evidence regarding the *Beryl G* hijacking was held in Victoria. The question before the court was simple: was there sufficient cause to send Paul Stromkins, Harry Sowash and Owen Baker to trial for the murder of Captain William Gillis? There was ample reason, the court decided. The trio were returned to Oakalla jail, and filed away in cells until the assizes started in June.

When June came, the murder trial was held in Victoria, the provincial capital. Sensation was guaranteed. The bodies of Gillis and his son had still not been found, but ghastly stories of their disposal were rife. Charlie Morris was still at home fighting extradition, leaving Paul Stromkins, Harry Sowash and Owen Baker to face the charge of murdering Captain Gillis. Proof of one murder was considered enough to hang all three—or would it be two?

Only minutes into the trial the courtroom audience was gasping. The prosecution declined to offer evidence against Paul Stromkins. His attorney rose and asked that his client be freed. The judge had no objection, and Stromkins stepped down from the dock, paid in full for the evidence he would give. And yet he stayed in jail! On the ferry to Victoria, Sergeant Bob Owens had been offered a bet by Sowash: $20 that neither he nor Baker would ever return to the cells of Oakalla. Were the words empty or had they a deeper meaning? Was Sowash expressing his confidence that they would be found not guilty or was it a hint that they were to be broken loose by rumrunning confederates? Tight security at the courthouse would take care of such an attempt, but there was another possibility. Could it be that Stromkins was about to meet a sudden end? Take away his evidence and the case would collapse. And then Sowash and Baker would go free, guilty or not. It was decided that until the trial was over Stromkins must be kept under guard in the courthouse lock-up.

When the trial began in earnest, witnesses from Canada and the United States testified at length. What emerged was a clear confirmation that American prohibition laws had been breached; a vital link, but what of murder? Knowledge of that was confined to those present when the deed was done.

Paul Stromkins was there—almost. He, Sowash, Baker and Morris had sailed from Cadboro Bay, out to make easy money, as darkness fell on September 15, 1924. Owen Baker had set the scene for them: "Pete Marinoff is shipping liquor and we know where his supply ship's going to be anchored. All we have to do is sail there and help ourselves." Off Sidney Island, all but Stromkins

Handcuffed and carrying a bag, "Cannonball" Baker begins a journey leading to the hangman. (*photo courtesy the Seattle Museum of History and Industry* [Seattle Post-Intelligencer *Collection*])

had rowed off in the dinghy in search of the anchored rum boat; he was left to bring the *Denman II* up to the *Beryl G* when her crew had been subdued. After fifteen minutes, Stromkins heard two gun shots. The silence washed back only to be broken some time later by Owen Baker splashing up in the dinghy. "Get going," he said. Stromkins started his engine and got going, and when the *Denman II* was tied alongside the *Beryl G* the transfer of the liquor cargo began. There was no sign of Captain Gillis, and to explain his absence, Charlie Morris told Stromkins, "We had to shoot the old man. We shot him a little in the arm." It was not true.

Paul Stromkins was a Polish immigrant, forced always to strive for the elusive English word that would best say what he meant. But there was more to his discomfort than language. As he spoke from the witness box, the pauses as he searched for words grew longer, he gripped the dock rail and his knuckles whitened, his voice shook and his face twisted as though he might burst into tears. Telling the first part of the story had been relatively easy recital but the part he hated to remember was approaching.

Prosecutor Archie Johnson nudged him on, "You must tell the court what you saw, Mr. Stromkins. All of it."

There was no escape. Paul Stromkins spoke, haltingly, unwillingly, torn by an emotional turmoil. "I saw young Gillis come on deck with Harry Sowash behind him. Then Harry's hand went up, and he brought something crashing down on the boy's head. The boy fell . . . he fell down on the deck . . . I saw him . . . I saw him move . . . once . . . and then he went still." Tears rolled unchecked down Stromkins' cheeks. For a while he was beyond speech.

The prosecutor urged him forward again, "Go on, Mr. Stromkins."

Paul Stromkins' hands gripped the witness box rails as he fought for control. "Morris and Baker came up from the cabin . . . they were carrying Captain Gillis. He was dead." Stromkins' voice was puzzled, as though he still didn't believe what he had seen. "They were dead . . . they were both dead . . . Gillis and his son . . . both of them," he wailed. "Oh! my God." Face in hands, he sobbed.

His ordeal was not yet over. The bodies had never been found. Where were they? Stromkins shuddered and went on with his testimony. The *Denman II* had headed for deep water, with the *Beryl G* and its sad cargo in tow. As they went Owen Baker had prepared the bodies for disposal. Gillis and his son would be together in death: Baker handcuffed them, a hand from each, tied a rope to the handcuffs, and to the rope's free end lashed an anchor. Then he crossed to the *Denman II*, hooking the anchor flukes over her stern rail as he passed. Casually, when the deepest part of the sea was below, he set the *Beryl G* adrift. As the distance between the boats grew, the line from the anchor to the bodies tightened and drew them slithering along the deck until they were dragged over the bow rail and lay rolling slackly in the swell like an obscene sea monster. Then Owen Baker unhooked the anchor from the stern of the *Denman II* and dropped it into the sea. The anchor headed for the sea floor taking with it the mortal remains of Captain Gillis and his son. As he ended his story Stromkins' voice became shrill with horror, "Oh! my God . . . Baker slashed the bodies with his knife so that they would sink more quickly!"

When it was their turn, the testimony of Baker and Sowash was divergent enough to have it appear that they might have been on different planets rather than together on Paul Stromkins' *Denman II* on the night when Captain Gillis and his son met their end. Indeed, so different were they in manner and appearance that it was difficult for those in the courtroom to imagine them working together in any venture.

Owen Baker oozed confidence when he stood in the witness stand and told his story. He was a stocky man, tough, and touched with arrogance. Dressed in a dark suit, he looked rather ordinary and had he been seated with the courtroom spectators no one would have paid him the slightest attention. Indeed, as he sat in the prisoner's dock it was difficult for many observers to see him as a murderer. His opening testimony was smooth. Most of the details surrounding his rumrunning exploits he admitted to freely. And why not? Apparent openness would serve him well—there would be no penalty imposed on him in Canada for breaking the prohibition laws of the United States. He had sailed on the *Denman II* with Stromkins, Sowash and Morris as others had already said. Leaving Cadboro Bay, on the eastern shore of Vancouver Island, at seven in the evening they had arrived at Anacortes on the Washington shore at seven the next morning. They had made no stops on the way. The events described by Stromkins and backed up by Sowash were, he claimed, pure imagination. Much had been made of the use of a gun and handcuffs. Baker insisted that he had never owned either in his entire life.

This was news to Pete Marinoff as he sat listening. Some years ago, while about his rumrunning affairs, his car had been stopped in Tacoma by a gun-wielding bandit who had relieved him of his liquid cargo and the contents of his wallet. To add to the indignity of such treatment, Marinoff and his companion had been left handcuffed. The miscreant turned out to be Owen Baker. No handcuffs? No gun? Baker had been sentenced to a term in prison for stealing the money—it would hardly have done to have complained about the loss of the bootlegged booze—and for his use of both gun and handcuffs. It was all in the public record. When the prosecutor asked "Cannonball" Baker if he had ever seen the *Beryl G*, he smirked and said that he had—six months after the alleged hijacking, the police had taken him to see her. Other than that, he had never set eyes on her. The prosecutor probed in vain. Owen Baker was admitting to nothing more. If there was gain to the prosecution it was in that the man on the stand at times came close to losing his temper and showed a truculent streak which suggested that crossing him would be unwise. Getting in a parting shot, Owen Baker said that it was possible that Sowash and Stromkins had gone to the *Beryl G* during the afternoon of September 15 and committed the crime of which he was being unjustly accused. Naturally, he had an iron-clad alibi for the entire afternoon.

When he appeared on the witness stand, Harry Sowash kept strictly to the contents of his original confession. He had no quarrel with Owen Baker's story up to the time of sailing from Cadboro Bay; beyond that point there was no comparison. Off Sidney Island, he, Baker and Charlie Morris had left the *Denman II* in the dinghy and rowed to the *Beryl G*. Morris and Baker had been armed; he had been unarmed. The armed pair had left the dinghy and boarded the rum transporter; he had stayed in the dinghy. Two shots had been fired. Later he had seen two bodies stretched out on the deck of the *Beryl G*. In deep water, near Halibut Island, Baker had dumped the bodies overboard weighted by an anchor. The drift of the story was clear: Morris and Baker had committed murder while he had occupied the dinghy some distance away; he had been a minor player under the malign influence of Owen Baker. Sowash had undoubtedly impressed some of the jury. He was younger than Baker, slightly built, used English well, spoke softly, and had none of Baker's abrasive edge. Violence and Harry Sowash seemed unlikely partners.

There were three versions of the fatal night's events. Who had told the truth? Baker? Sowash? Stromkins? Certainly not all of them. Possibly none of them. The emotional evidence of Paul Stromkins had been dramatic in the extreme. Too dramatic? "How could the evidence of such an emotionally unbalanced man be believed?" asked the attorneys of Sowash and Baker. And there was another weakness, they claimed, which undermined the whole case. What of the bodies? Could men be found guilty of murder when the fact of murder had not been proven?

Before they left to consider their verdict, the judge put the jury straight on the matter of bodies. That the police had failed to find the bodies of the men allegedly murdered was not their first concern. "You must," he said, wagging his bewigged head for emphasis, "erase that fact from your minds. The prosecution has shown that it is possible to dispose of a body at sea in a way that would preclude any hope of it ever being found." What need concern them was that men, without exception, are responsible for their own conduct and must pay a penalty if the results transgressed the law. It was easy for the judge to talk in his dry, legalistic way, but how could the jury members so easily forget? Theirs was the hard part; that of determining guilt or innocence while the shadow of the gallows hung over their deliberations. The temptation of using the lack of bodies as a loophole to justify a not-guilty verdict would be strong in men reluctant to see others hang.

Outside the courthouse, the sun shone and all seemed well with the world. But inside the building, the atmosphere was tense. In a room set apart, twelve jurors debated matters of life and death. In the courtroom awaiting the jury verdict were two women, sitting apart, avoiding eye contact, yet closely linked. One woman, widow of the late Captain William Gillis, had suffered the double loss of her son and husband. The other woman, pale and distraught, was the wife of Owen "Cannonball" Baker. Whether or not she would soon join Mrs. Gillis in widowhood hung in the balance.

For Mrs. Gillis all hope was gone. For Mrs. Baker a tag-end of hope remained.

Time passed slowly. Courtroom spectators talked together quietly, as though raised voices were inappropriate. Some stood uneasily by the panelled walls. Some sat passively, eyes blank. Others tiptoed out and walked the halls. But no one strayed far. Several times there were whispers of the jury's imminent return. Whispering an untruth doesn't make it true. The jury was out and stayed out. Time dragged. Would the jury never decide? Then the lawyers bustled in. Now the whisper was true. The jury had decided.

It was shortly before noon when two manacled men were led into the courtroom and seated in the prisoner's dock. Then all present stood at a court official's command as the judge took his place. The silence was intense. The jury, stone-faced, trooped in. The trial had lasted a week. Its conclusion took only minutes. In answer to a question from the judge, the jury foreman answered that the accused had been found guilty of murder. No mercy had been shown to the murdered men; none was recommended for the murderers. Judge Morrison wasted no time. His message to Owen Baker and Harry Sowash was plain, "I direct that you be taken to the prison from which you came and that on Friday, September 4, you be hanged by the neck until you are dead."

Charlie Morris crossed into Canada on the day the death sentence was passed. His fight against extradition had been shorter than anticipated.

At his trial, he told a startlingly simple version of the events of the night of the *Beryl G* raid; if it could be called a version of events. He had boarded the *Denman II* along with Owen Baker. That he remembered, though fuzzily. He had been drinking all day and was not at his best. As soon as the *Denman II* had pulled away from the shore he had curled up by the warm engine and gone to sleep. When he awoke, they were only a mile or two from Anacortes. That was it. He remembered nothing of the trip. Not a thing. Paul Stromkins, as hysterical as ever when he gave his testimony, was kinder to Morris than he had been to Sowash and Baker. He made no suggestion that Morris had killed anyone. But did that matter? The jury thought not; as an accomplice, Morris shared the guilt. The recommendation to mercy was brushed aside by the judge. Charlie Morris was sentenced to hang. By another coincidence his sentence was announced on the day that the first appeal of Sowash and Morris was denied.

The pair had been unlucky to lose their appeal, but lucky that it had been heard at all. For some inexplicable reason, their foot-dragging lawyers had delayed appealing until three weeks before the day fixed for them to hang. Notice of appeal automatically stayed the execution date, or so the lawyers thought. Not so, said the warden of Oakalla jail; he had orders to hang the pair on September 4 and would do so unless a court of appeal said otherwise. Unfortunately, the court of appeal was not due to meet again until after the execution date. The lawyers, furiously working the legal levers, managed to persuade a judge to grant a temporary reprieve.

When they did meet, the British Columbia court of appeal judges decided, by a vote of three to two, that they had no reason to interfere with the decision of the lower court. A new hanging date was set. The judges of the Supreme Court of Canada heard the next appeal and declined to order a new trial. Another door had been closed, but a glimmer of hope remained. The federal cabinet could override the courts. Could, but refused to do so. The end of the appeal system had been reached and Sowash and Baker must hang. But Charlie Morris managed to wriggle clear, his death sentence was commuted to life imprisonment.

At dawn on January 14, 1926, two hooded figures stood on a raised wooden platform. Near them stood Arthur Ellis, fruit farmer and public hangman. It was to the hangman that Baker said his final words, "Step on her, kid. Make it quick."

He did. With a crash, two trapdoors opened. Where Harry Sowash and Owen Baker had stood a split second before only taut, vibrating ropes were visible. It was over.

Greed had brought them to the gallows, and the rum trade had provided the setting. Rumrunning was rough, but on the west coast usually kept within reasonably civilized bounds. This had been different.

Pete Marinoff had wanted a stern message passed on to potential hijackers.

The hangman had obliged.

5
GIVE THE MAN A GOLD WATCH

Newly delivered from near destruction, by the grace of God and his own never-say-die seamanship, Captain Jalmar Granman sat wearily on the Astoria dock and told his story of peril at sea. He had, he said, cast off from Willapa on the Washington shore early on Sunday morning with the *Gray's Harbor* loaded below and above decks with a cargo of lumber to be delivered to the docks of San Francisco. It was not a pleasant morning. Low, scudding clouds and sudden sweeping sheets of rain suggested that the voyage would be no more enjoyable than many other winter voyages he had made. Yet, for all that, picking his way through the treacherous waters of Willapa Bay had not been much different than usual. But once across the bar between Cape Shoalwater and the northern tip of the Long Beach Peninsula, things had rapidly worsened. In the open ocean, a southerly gale, that would blow harder before it subsided, shrieked in fury. The sea had many moods; this mood, like all the others, had to be faced. For professional seamen there was no turning back. When well clear of the shore, Captain Granman turned the blunt bows of the *Gray's Harbor* directly into the storm and set out to cross the mouth of the Columbia River.

By one o'clock in the afternoon his ship was twenty-seven miles south of the Columbia River Lightship, taking a heavy pounding and leaking badly. Close by, and in an even worse state, was the twenty-year-old *Caoba*, a 579-ton coastal freighter driven by a four-hundred-horsepower steam engine. Both ships had left Willapa at the same time and had been in each other's sight throughout the day.

Captain Granman's listeners knew the sea; they nodded understandingly as he told how he had refused the request of Captain Sandvig to take the *Caoba* in tow. What was the point? The strongest hawser linking the two wildly bucking ships could never have stood the strain. They also knew why, in spite of his misgivings and at the insistence of the *Caoba*'s captain, he had changed his mind and made the attempt. Ships in danger of foundering cannot be left to sink; men in danger at sea cannot be left to die.

The listeners, visualizing the tumultuous scene from Granman's modest words, recognized the fine seamanship required to get a line on board the troubled ship. First, one end of a light line had been bent to the end of a hawser and to its other end a lifebelt attached. Then the lifebelt had been dropped over the stern, and with the line streaming behind his ship, Granman had steamed across the bows of the *Caoba* and let the line drift back to her. A deft dip with a boathook snagged the line, and the hawser was pulled aboard the water-logged ship and made fast. Nearing four o'clock in the afternoon, the linked duo set course for Astoria, a safe port—across the bar and well sheltered within the banks of the Columbia River. While the *Caoba* still had power, the tow went well. But, within minutes, rising water doused her boilers and left her wallowing helplessly. The dead weight stretched the tow-line to its limits and then a sudden lurch exceeded those limits and the hawser snapped. By that time the distressed ship had nine feet of sea water sloshing in her holds and only the deck cargo of timber, straining to free itself from its lashings, was holding her afloat.

The *Gray's Harbor* stayed in position, circling the *Caoba* until nine in the evening. Then Captain Granman decided that for his crew's safety he must run for port alone. All six of his mechanical pumps were working at top speed and the water in his own holds was still rising. The buoyancy with which his ship had previously ridden the waves was markedly reduced. Each time she slipped into the trough of a wave, it seemed unlikely that she would ever rise to the crest of the one close behind. It was ironic that while the *Caoba* was being held above the surface by her deck cargo the *Gray's Harbor* was near to foundering under the weight of hers. When Granman's decision to leave was passed to Sandvig, the *Caoba*'s skipper asked that his crew be taken off the sinking ship. Granman had tried but the task was impossible. It would have been madness to launch small boats in such a sea. A hint of self-justification crept into the captain's voice—he had left a sinking ship and hated to admit it. But his audience of experienced seamen were hardly likely to accuse him of cowardice. Sailing away, he had ordered the cargo lashings let go. Yet, in spite of the gyrations of the ship, the deck cargo refused to move until the weary crew jettisoned it by hand, littering the heaving sea with sawn lumber.

Just before four o'clock the next morning, Captain Granman carefully positioned his ship within hailing distance of the Columbia River Lightship and yelled a message about the plight of the *Caoba*. To be sure that the watch-keeper had understood, Granman had him repeat back the message. Several hours later he had asked for confirmation that the message had been sent to the shore. It had not. Beside himself with rage, Captain Granman left no doubt that it must be sent—and quickly. It was, and when the radio message was received in Astoria, the coast guard vessel *Algonquin* put to sea without a minute wasted.

Fate was kind. After an anxious wait for the shore-bound watchers, the pilot cutter *Cudahy* landed nine of the *Caoba*'s crew on the Astoria dock. The *Algonquin* delivered the rest. The coast guard cutter had, or so it appeared, been able to combine its rescue mission with regular business. Led by the nose, the *Pescawha*, a rumrunner of Canadian registry, trailed behind.

As told by the British Columbia press, the capture had come about through the rumrunners' devotion to the highest traditions of the sea. Captain Robert Pamphlet, tossing in the storm in his old converted fishing craft, had seen the foundering *Caoba* and in a fine feat of seamanship had rescued her entire crew. That was not enough. The Canadian captain had then decided to land his American guests on home ground and he headed for shore. That was unwise. Within the territorial waters of the United States, the *Pescawha* and coast guard cutter *Algonquin* had met. The cutter's crew were delighted to take on board the rescued men. But they also took Pamphlet, his ship, cargo and crew. Rumrunners were

U.S.C.G. cutter *Algonquin*, captor of the *Pescawha* and Captain Pamphlet. *(photo courtesy of the Coast Guard Museum, Seattle)*

not welcome within the twelve-mile limit. With fine seamanship repaid by base ingratitude, the story of Captain Pamphlet and the *Pescawha* took on mythical overtones. In fact, the first Canadian report had unknowingly departed from the truth.

Captain Granman had ended his story of the plight of the *Caoba* with a hope that her crew had been picked up by a passing vessel that, having no radio, had been unable to report the fact. Of one thing he was certain: the crew would not have taken to the lifeboats. In his opinion, only madmen would have considered such a thing on a night like that.

True, madmen might have unshipped the lifeboats without thought: but a sane man might have thought long and hard and still done it. In fact, Captain Sandvig, having as his only remaining alternative staying on a ship that was certain to sink, had ordered his crew into the two available lifeboats.

News of the abandonment of the Caoba came from the captain of the steamer *Forest King*. He had found the deserted vessel with her lifeboats gone and ropes dangling loose from the davits. Mindful of salvage possibilities, he had taken her in tow. As Captain Granman had already found, there was no hope of success. In the turbulent seas, the tow-line parted. The *Forest King* resumed course and left the scene. A final radio message reported that the *Caoba*, derelict and a menace to navigation, was ten miles west of North Head, Washington. Of the lifeboats there was no sign.

It was an anxious time in Astoria, but spirits were raised when the *Cudahy* brought in nine *Caoba* survivors; exhausted men who had ridden mountainous waves in an open boat for thirty-eight hours. What news had they of their missing shipmates? Not much. The *Caoba*'s lifeboats had drifted apart. When last seen, the occupants of the other lifeboat, captain included, had been in good health and spirits.

Had been. Each passing hour of exposure would be whittling away their chance of survival.

Yet, almost as they spoke, another drama was being played out over the storm-lashed horizon. The men of the Canadian vessel *Pescawha* had found the second lifeboat—and not with any great delight. According to one of the rescued men, the sailors of the *Pescawha*, fearful of hijackers, were lying flat upon the deck with heavy rifles trained as their open boat approached. But once the situation was explained there was no holding back. The rumrunner carried a crew of six and had accommodations to match. In an instant the numbers on board almost tripled as Captain Sandvig, Chief Engineer John Lycett, Second Mate Paul Toomey, First Assistant Engineer K.A. Young, Crewmen Dan Fairfield, Carl Petersen, William Christensen, Isaac Nielson and Jose Rodriguez gauged the relative movements of the two vessels, took their chances and scrambled over the bulwarks of the *Pescawha*. And there was one more of the *Caoba*'s crew to be counted—the ship's cat, undoubtedly lacking some of its original nine lives, had also survived. The rescued men were wet, tired, hungry and thirsty. Seeing to their needs was the first order of business. Speaking of the warmth of their reception, Captain Sandvig said, "They treated us like kings. Everything on board was ours. They gave us their food, their clothes, their bunks and their booze."

Then the coast guard cutter *Algonquin* showed up. Her captain, informed by radio that the *Caoba* had been abandoned, was now searching for the second lifeboat. And there it was, trailing behind a black-hulled vessel with an ugly red deck-house that looked for all the world like "a section hand's shanty beside a railroad." It was not a very flattering description of the *Pescawha*, but Captain Pamphlet allowed little time for critical examination of her lines. Immediately the *Algonquin* was sighted, he turned his schooner from a course set to deliver his passengers ashore to due west and headed for the open sea as fast as his engine could propel him. The captain of the *Algonquin* gave chase. It became a toss up whether the cutter would catch up with the *Pescawha* or the weak February sun dip below the horizon and bring darkness to aid Pamphlet's escape. Calls to halt brought no response. When it seemed that the setting sun would win the race, a shot was fired across the *Pescawha*'s bows. This was serious business. Too many lives were at stake to make the thought of defiance possible. Without hesitation, Captain Pamphlet cut his engine and, as his vessel wallowed in the swell, took up his megaphone and yelled, "Don't fire, I have shipwrecked seamen aboard."

Under the cover of the *Algonquin*'s guns, a party was sent out to inspect the *Pescawha*. Her liquor cargo was soon found. It was no business of the United States government, Pamphlet insisted. He was outside territorial limits and was on a high-seas passage from Canada to a destination in Mexico. Could he prove his destination? He could not—or would not. The launch returned to the *Algonquin* with four of the *Caoba*'s crew as passengers and narrowly escaped being swamped. The rest of the rescued men went across to the coast guard cutter in the *Caoba*'s lifeboat. The captain of the cutter refused to believe Pamphlet's claim of a Canada-to-Mexico voyage. Clearly, the man was a rumrunner. The *Pescawha*'s liquor load filled not a quarter of her hold. That a vessel would sail for Mexico with so much wasted space made no sense. More likely than not, she had been lurking off the coast for a considerable time, off-loading liquor orders to American boats. Captain Wilshaar placed the *Pescawha* and her crew under arrest and ordered Captain Pamphlet to make fast the *Algonquin*'s hawser to his bow. Pamphlet, having no reason to want to assist in the capture of his own vessel, refused. However, he made no resistance when a boarding party was put on board to manage the tow.

It was a great day for Astoria when the men of the *Caoba* arrived. Tragedy at sea had been averted, and not least by the part played by Pamphlet and his crew. When they went ashore, those present, led by Captain Sandvig and his crew, cheered wildly.

There was no doubt of the feelings of the sea faring community towards those they thought unfairly placed under arrest, and the words of a *Caoba* crew member put it best, "We cannot help but feel that they are now prisoners because of their humanity to us. They may be bootleggers *but they are men.*"

The local newspapers were hard pressed to draw a balance between all those deserving of praise.

Captain Sandvig, at thirty years of age a mere babe as a ship's commander, had handled a difficult situation well. He had led his men with firmness and skill. Had he cracked under the strain, the survival of his crew would have been extremely doubtful.

And Captain Granman of the *Gray's Harbor* had also done well. He, together with his crew, had stood by the *Caoba* far longer than prudence suggested was safe or reasonable. Had Granman not passed a message to the lightship about the *Caoba's* difficulties, the search might have been delayed until far too late for success.

An imaginative reporter stumbled upon Sir Francis Drake, a British sea dog not above piratical behavior when the occasion suited him, as a somewhat inappropriate role model for the law-enforcers of the *Algonquin*. "The rumrunning schooner *Pescawha* was laid by the heels in a stern chase," he wrote, "such as Sir Francis Drake sailed off this coast long ago, and it was brought to port at the end of a ten-inch Manila hawser with a prize crew at her helm . . . ." Drake, no doubt, had traditions to uphold and so did modern sailors. In the opinion of the reporter "the officers of the coast guard cutter *Algonquin* upheld the fine traditions of the U.S. Coast Guard and penned another shining page which will embellish the proud record of their ancient service."

But there were other traditions of the sea which had been upheld and editorial comment mentioned them. The "noble response of Captain Pamphlet and his men," the editor of the *Astoria Evening Standard* wrote, "subordinated personal considerations to a duty imposed upon them by humanitarian impulses." That fact marked them as real men. But then a sanctimonious note crept in: "real men and worthy of a better calling than that in which they are engaged"

There was a point of conflict. How did the upholding of the coast guard tradition of service at sea measure up to the upholding of the humanitarian sea going tradition of common sailors like Captain Pamphlet and his crew? Many admirers of the rumrunning crew had nothing good to say of the *Algonquin* and its controlling authorities. How could they hold the *Pescawha*'s crew on such a trivial matter when they had saved American lives? If it came to that, how could the seafarers of the *Algonquin* reconcile their police action with the greater good that had been done. The editor answered that Captain Wilshaar and his men, "doubtless were tempted to ignore the contraband cargo." However, that was a choice not open to them. "As soldiers of the United States, taught in a school of stern discipline, their duty was too plain to be canceled by personal desire. They, too, upheld old and honored tradition."

There were also those with no scruples about prosecuting the crew of the *Pescawha*. A rumrunner was a rumrunner and deserved to be treated as such. The war against rumrunners had been long, hard and often unsuccessful. The pendulum, swinging too frequently to the rumrunners' side, was showing signs of swinging towards the forces of law and order. The vessel had played into their hands, and the opportunity to pass a strong message could not be ignored on the trifling grounds of sentimentality. Captain Robert Pamphlet and Mate S. Bridges, along with deckhands G.H. Rex, William Tickle, J. Silverson and Pete Kinney, were charged with violating the liquor laws of the United States. Possibly that charge would not be sufficient to assure conviction. On instructions from the federal capital, a district immigration inspector on the spot laid two additional charges— entering a United States port without inspection and not having an immigration visa. Nothing was said of the involuntary aspect of their entry; towed in by a government vessel regardless of all protests. In spite of their difficulties, the captain and crew of the *Pescawha* remained remarkably cheerful. To some of the *Caoba*'s crew, bemoaning the circumstances that had caused the problem, one of the accused rumrunners said, "Don't feel bad, mates, we did it and we'd do it again to save a seaman's life." Captain Pamphlet was philosophical. There was no bitterness in his voice when he commented that what had happened was to be expected in the fortunes of the trade in which he was engaged. But he still insisted that he was outside the American territorial limits when his boat was commandeered. The lifeboat survivors agreed, but the authorities were not impressed. The likelihood

of men who had been engaged on a desperate struggle for survival, both on their sinking ship and then in a storm-tossed
lifeboat, knowing their precise position was extremely low.

The American government was displeased with the Rum
Row situation. It was beyond their ability to control. But if they
could not adequately police those involved, they could at least
make conditions more awkward for those who would thumb
their noses at the laws designed to keep the United States dry.
Diplomatic pressure on the British government helped. In May,
1924, a treaty was signed which effectively replaced the internationally agreed three-mile limit as far as the two signatories were
concerned. His Britannic Majesty agreed that no objection would
be raised by his government if private vessels sailing under the
red ensign were boarded outside the international limit when
there was reasonable grounds for suspicion that an attempt was
being made to import alcoholic beverages into the United States
in violation of its laws. If the suspicions were proved to be accurate, the British government would have no complaint if such a
ship was seized and taken to a United States port to await further action by an American court. The legal limits were not
indefinite: neither were they precise. The general limit was set at
twelve nautical miles, but a rider was added—or a distance that
can be traversed in one hour by the vessel concerned. There was
grist for the lawyers' mill; how many factors can change the
distance covered in one hour. There is a theoretical limit: the
vessel's best speed. There is a practical limit imposed by the sea,
the state of the ship at a particular time, the load being carried—
and a hundred other things. Proof would be difficult either way.
And there was another item in the agreement that could make a
slow ship fast: "In cases, however, in which the liquor is intended
to be conveyed to the United States, its territories or possessions
by a vessel other then the one boarded and searched, it shall be
the speed of such other vessel and not the speed of the vessel
boarded which shall determine the distance from the coast at
which the right of this article shall be exercised." At its most
ridiculous, that meant that if a man in a rowboat passed a bottle
of rum to a powerful rumrunning motorboat, the speed of the
rowboat could be legally argued to be as much as forty knots. In
real terms, it meant that every supply ship on Rum Row could be
assumed to have a speed far in excess of its true capability and

as a result its cruising distance from the coast would have to be adjusted seaward. And this to the advantage of the United States Coast Guard.

How did this affect Captain Pamphlet? As a Canadian, he sailed under the red ensign, therefore, the limit for him was at least twelve miles. It was claimed that he had been found within that relatively new limit. If that was true, he could expect little useful help from his own country or its motherland.

On the river off Astoria, coast guard men tested the speed potential of the *Pescawha*. Her top speed was supposed to be somewhere around five or six knots; the coast guard claimed that her speed was unusually fast. The implication was that even if she had been outside the twelve-mile limit when boarded, given her speed and the length of time spent on the chase, she must have started from well within the limit. The thousand-case liquor cargo of the *Pescawha* was the biggest catch made off the Columbia mouth to that time, and the prohibition agents were determined to make the most of their unusual opportunity. Had Captain Pamphlet lived today, he would have done well in public relations. Through newspaper interviews he offered Captain Wilshaar, of the *Algonquin*, an apology for being so uncooperative at the time of his capture. "I felt that I should maintain an aloofness and laissez-faire policy. I had to tell Captain Wilshaar that I had no manifest, and I declined to make his hawser fast to my vessel, not from desire to impede him but because I wanted to do nothing to prejudice my interests and those of my men." To those men determined to make him pay for sinning against the liquor laws of the United States, he offered thanks. "I want to express my thanks to you, customs commissioners, and other officers with whom I have been dealing. I have been well and kindly treated." Soft words, possibly meant to turn aside wrath.

In a sense, the genial Robert Pamphlet had come home. "You know, my grandfather was at one time the boss of Astoria," he told a reporter. "John Dunn, my mother's father, was the Hudson's Bay Company factor from 1836 to 1840. He was dismissed by the HBC, I presume because he was too honest," he added with a smile. The fifty-two-year-old seaman had continued a family tradition by following a seafaring career. Eight years previously his father had died, the oldest active ship's captain on the Pacific coast. His brother was still serving as the chief engineer on the Grand

Trunk Pacific's SS *Prince George*. There was no doubt that Pamphlet had the sympathy of most of the people of the port of Astoria where such a family record would be admired. But the general admiration did not stay the charges against him and his crew.

Waiving the formality of a preliminary hearing in Astoria, the alleged rumrunners were sent to Portland where they had no difficulty in raising bail: $5,000 for Captain Pamphlet and $1,000 for crew members Bridges, Rex, Tickle, Silverson and Kinney on the rumrunning charge, and an additional $1,000 each for landing on United States territory illegally. It came to a large sum, but, no doubt, interested individuals with plenty of money were backing them.

While the initial moves in the legal chess match were being made, the *Pescawha* was sailed up the Columbia River and tied up at a wharf in Portland. Under heavy guard, her illicit cargo was unloaded, placed in trucks, and taken to secure vaults in the customs house. There was need for security. On arrival in Portland there were twenty-seven fewer cases of confiscated liquor on board than had been counted during the first check at Astoria.

The capture of the largest cargo of booze ever seized off the Oregon coast was big news, and there was an unusual feature that made it even bigger. An *Oregon Screen Review* cameraman, C. S. Piper, had sailed on the coast guard cutter *Algonquin* during its search for the missing *Caoba* crew. With a seaman hanging onto each leg of his camera tripod and two more seamen, "sea legs spread to brace themselves against the crashing waves," holding him in position, he had steadily turned the crank of his primitive movie camera and filmed the taking of the *Pescawha*. It was an historic day in news reporting, and only hours later the Rivoli Theater in Portland was backing up its main film, *Abraham Lincoln*, with what was being proudly advertised as the most remarkable film ever shot at sea.

While this was going on, the *Caoba* was still afloat—just. Paul Thompson, master of the tug *Douty*, found her tossing in the surf off Willapa Bay and managed to get a line on board. It was a manoeuvre that had almost cost him a man. Herman Nelson, mate of the tug, who had boarded the *Caoba* to secure the towline, had been forced to swim back to the *Douty* through heavy seas. It was a waste of effort. As Thompson headed for the entrance to the Columbia River, the wind increased its speed until it was blowing at over sixty miles an hour, raising tumultuous seas. In spite of the grim conditions, the bar was crossed safely and success seemed within reach when the hawser connecting the two ships suddenly parted. As Captain Thompson watched, the *Caoba* washed onto the sands of Peacock Spit. Within minutes the waves pounding the beach had washed over her and removed both funnel and deckhouse. Within weeks nothing but her boiler was left on the sands. The ship was no more, but the events that had led to its end would bring grief far into the future.

The news of Pamphlet's capture had traveled fast: the legal system seemed not to be making any progress at all. Four months had passed when the *Portland Spectator* demanded that Captain Pamphlet should be pardoned and the *Pescawha* released. It was unconscionable that charges had been laid and no action taken for four months. The newspaper reminded readers of the events that had led to the taking of both man and ship and recalled more civilized times: "when a rover by land or a rover by sea performed a deed of heroism, a pardon was at once granted the gallant outlaw, no matter how many and how serious had been his malefactions." But Pamphlet, who had put the *Pescawha* about to respond to the distress signals of the foundering *Caoba* and rescued from certain death nine of her crew, "found that in earning a hero's reward he had incurred a felon's fate."

The writer had nothing but praise for Pamphlet who had gone beyond the great love shown by those willing to lay down their lives for others. The story was an epic of the ravenous sea, splendid and inspiring. What of the boys of Canada and the United States who had been thrilled by Captain Pamphlet's splendid feat? Were they not entitled to a hero unsoiled by indictment or prosecution?

The myth was made. In reality, Captain Pamphlet had, by chance, picked up nine men from an open lifeboat. Or so Astoria and Portland newspapers had reported at the time. Now the story was very different. The *Pescawha* had responded to a signal from the sinking *Caoba*. In truth, the *Caoba* had no radio with which to signal. The crew of the *Pescawha*, described as standing by the *Caoba*, never saw her. When picked up, Captain Sandvig and the crew members accompanying him had been tossing in their lifeboat for the best part of two days. Truth and perceptions of the truth often vary. In the case of Robert Pam-

phlet, it is certain that this newer, more satisfactory story provided Canadian and American citizens with a very different view
from which to observe and form opinions of the trial—if and
when it ever got under way.

Alas for the boys of the United States and Canada, it did get
under way, and Captain Robert Pamphlet and his crew were
found guilty. Robert Pamphlet declined to run away. He had
been granted a twenty-day stay until his sentence began. When
it was over he left Canada, where he might have stayed without
much danger of facing extradition, reported to the authorities in
Portland and was imprisoned.

In May 1928, with four months of his sentence in McNeil
Island Prison behind him, Captain Pamphlet returned to a Portland courtroom to give evidence in the continuing saga of whether
the Canadian owners or the United States government should have
the *Pescawha*. To friendly reporters, he quipped, "Oh, everything
is lovely." Prison, it seemed was a good place to get an education. "I shall class my visit there as part of my schooling," he said.
"An education in the varieties of human beings." Questioned about
his fellow prisoners, he categorized them neatly. "Probably 30 percent are 'half and half' gentlemen, a combination of good and bad.
At least 30 percent are thorough 'rotters.' And the remaining 40
percent 'are all right sorts of fellows.'" He appreciated the regular
hours and the fresh air. He had some responsibility. "I have charge
of the tool house," he said with a smile. "I suppose I could be
converted into a plumber or a carpenter, but I believe that when my
two years' visit is ended I shall return to the sea in some capacity."

There were many who wished to help Captain Pamphlet cut
short his prison education and worked to have him freed. The
Vancouver *Province* newspaper had no quarrel with the right of
the United States to jail Robert Pamphlet. But it was a question
beyond simple legality. The instinct of the common man was
that the story of Captain Pamphlet and the *Pescawha* was not
one about which Canada should feel shame. In British Columbia,
the majority of the population believed that the circumstances of
his case entitled him to special treatment. The *Province*'s editorial
writer thought it not too late; if the right persons were to make
representations his release could yet be secured. The fact that
President Hoover had just been elected and might wish to culti-
vate the good will of Canada by an act of executive clemency in

Robert Pamphlet's case was a strengthening factor. Seeing the way the political wind was blowing, Attorney General Manson of British Columbia, while making it clear that he was not acting with any sympathy for the rumrunning business, undertook to lay all the facts of the case before the federal government. Nothing came of it. South of the border in Washington and Oregon, petitions for the release of Captain Pamphlet were signed by thousands of angry people and sent to the national capital. Nothing came of the petitions, either.

Captain Pamphlet was jinxed. And so were many rumrunning vessels including his own. The *Beryl G*, on which Captain Gillis and his son had died at the hands of Harry Sowash and Owen Baker, was a case in point. Long after Sowash and Baker had died on the gallows of Oakalla Prison, she lay unwanted at a Vancouver wharf. She was later purchased, and on a black night off Valdez Island, she struck a jagged reef and broke up. Few would have known that she was gone had it not been for a newspaper headline, "The *Beryl G* Comes To a Bad End." She had met her fate, renamed the *Manzanetta*. The change of name had not removed the jinx. The *Pescawha* also met a sad end. Confiscated by the United States government, the boat languished in a Portland dock until she was sold privately. The new owner seemed not to know what to do with her, and she fared no better under several subsequent owners. Eventually, Victor Riley converted her into a whale catcher of sorts with a deck-mounted car engine of dubious reliability as an auxiliary power source. The voyage he set out on in late February 1933 was an ill-conceived venture pushed beyond prudent safety limits. As the *Pescawha* headed out from the mouth of the Columbia River into the teeth of a raging south-westerly gale, the auxiliary engine died, and the vessel started to drift towards the long arm of the north jetty. The lifeboat, knocked from its davits by a massive wave, crushed the skipper and he went overboard. Considering the size of the waves pounding the jagged boulders of the jetty, it was remarkable that any of the crew survived, but they did by clinging to whatever pieces of driftwood they could grab. Captain Riley's body was recovered a few days later, appropriately in Deadman's Bay. The *Pescawha* was matchwood. Only her wheel was cast ashore as a reminder that she had ever existed. She had failed to outlast prohibition in the United States by less than a year.

But before his ship was dead and gone, so was Captain Robert Pamphlet. In September 1931 a newspaper headline carried his obituary. Released from jail at the end of August 1929, he returned to Canada, and two years later died at the home of his brother, after an illness of several months. The cause of death was tuberculosis, a souvenir, it is said, of his stay in McNeil Island Penitentiary. He was fifty-eight years old. All that can be said with assurance of Robert Pamphlet's association with the *Pescawha* and rumrunning is that it brought him fame as a seaman—fame and a gold watch.

The watch, presented to him by those who owed him a great deal and admired him for his devotion to the code of the sea, was inscribed:

> Captain Robert Pamphlet, a true sailor,
> in recognition of his action in rescuing
> the crew of our SS *Caoba* at sea,
> February 3, 1925.
>   Sudden & Christensen

The *Vancouver Sun*, eulogizing him after death, echoed and expanded the brief words of the inscription:

> *It was always the opinion of a great many people, in that country (the United States) as well as in Canada, that he should never have been convicted. It was the opinion of a great many more that, having been convicted, he should have been pardoned. Technically and legally, he went to prison because he was a rumrunner taken with his ship. Actually he went to prison because he put the covenant of the sea and the honour of the good seaman before his own safety and risked his life and his freedom to rescue American sailors in peril. He was a rumrunner by ill chance or necessity. He was a true man by the virtue of his own good character. They ought to have found a better way of dealing with him than to make him a companion of felons.*

It was a fitting epitaph.

6
THE DRY NAVY STRIKES BACK

Passing Port Townsend, at the entrance to Puget Sound, in late January 1925, Pete Marinoff was hailed by government rum chasers and ordered to stop. He ignored the order and opened up the twin throttles of his speedboat to maximum power. A warning shot was fired. Marinoff kept going. The rum chasers were fast, well armed, and not at all reluctant to use their armament. Over the crack of their one-pounder cannon was stitched the rapid chatter of Lewis machine-guns. After fifteen miles of dodging shot and shell, Pete Marinoff closed his throttles. By this time his cargo had been dumped overboard, and there was no reason to flee. As the rum chasers pulled alongside, he called cheerfully, "What's all the shooting about, boys?" They answered by arresting him and confiscating his boat. Having no evidence of rumrunning, the coast guard charged him with a breach of the navigation regulations—he had no running lights. And then they added a charge of conspiring to break the prohibition laws. Conspiring was easier to prove than was rumrunning when the evidence was at the bottom of the sea. Life was becoming tough for rumrunners. After years of nail-biting frustration, the United States Coast Guard, better known as the "Dry Navy," was becoming aggressive.

At the start of national prohibition, the commandant of the

Seventy-five footers ("six-bitters") of the U.S.C.G. moored at Port Townsend. (*photo courtesy of the Coast Guard Museum, Seattle*)

service had promised that large numbers of men would be quickly trained to sail the modern vessels of an expanded fleet. The coast guard was the place to be for ambitious sailors looking for quick promotion. It was an optimistic forecast, and wildly inaccurate. Politicians, quick to make demands on the coast guard, were slow to vote the funds to get things done. The promised expansion was a long, bitter struggle.

But persistence paid. At the time of Pete Marinoff's embarrassment, swarms of custom-designed vessels were entering the battle. Thirty-six footers capable of twenty-five knots were on hand for coastal patrols against high-speed rumrunners. Seventy-five footers, known as "six-bitters," were coming into service to be used against law-breakers with more modest equipment. "Dollar" and "dollar and a quarter" boats, hundred footers and 125 footers were being commissioned. Steel-hulled and powered by twin diesels, they could stay at sea for up to a month. With a 3.25-inch-calibre gun mounted forward and Lewis machine-guns at hand, both sizes of vessel were useful for shadowing the mother ships of Rum Row and discouraging illicit liquor transfers to shore-bound boats.

New boats had brought new tactics. The gloves were off. When the *Pescawha* had been captured off the mouth of the Columbia River, claims were made that the vessel was well outside internationally agreed limits. Perhaps that was true, perhaps not. No matter. The American authorities were no longer inclined to go to the trouble of catching a rumrunning boat only to free it for such a trifling reason. The jurisdiction of the United States over the waters off its shores now seemed to be as elastic as circumstances demanded. Perhaps the forcible towing of the liquor supply ship *Quadra* from international waters to San Francisco harbour, before the *Pescawha* incident occurred, had been the first act of a new policy.

In 1924 the *Quadra* was thirty-three years old. Built for the Canadian government, the vessel had been used as a lighthouse tender, a ferry for important visitors, a coastal patrol vessel, a fisheries enforcement vessel, and a survey ship. In 1917 the *Quadra* started a slow decline. Entering Nanaimo harbour in a thick fog, she collided with another ship and sank. Salvaged, she became on ore carrier, endlessly steaming between the Britannia Mines on Howe Sound and the port of Tacoma. In 1924 the vessel was sold by the mining company and became part of the rum fleet. The *Quadra*, cleared for Mexico with a cargo of liquor, cruised Rum Row opposite San Francisco and, by arrangement, off-loaded portions of her alcoholic cargo to fast motor launches which headed for the shore. It was dull work, but profitable. Each departing load earned huge profits for the businessmen of the rum trade. Profits that had already been boosted by the simple expedient of having declared a false destination. Liquor destined for Mexico was free of export duty. On liquor honestly declared to be destined for the United States, export duty was levied. For a trifling sum per case, corrupt Mexican officials would happily send documents to the ship's owners to prove that the cargo had been off-loaded at Ensenada.

Sometimes the *Quadra* replenished her liquor stock from a larger supply ship. It was during such a restocking that she was holed, when a heavy ocean swell tossed her against the hull of the *Malahat*. Watch-keeping suffered while the crew plugged the hole, and when they next looked around, the United States Coast Guard cutter *Shawnee* was within easy firing range. The rumrunning career of a ship that had been carrying ore earlier in the year was about to come to an abrupt end. But first, the ritual dance had to be played out.

The *Shawnee*'s captain ordered the *Quadra* to heave to. The *Quadra*'s captain, naturally, refused to obey. As a warning of what further disobedience would bring, a shot was fired across the *Quadra*'s bows. It was time to take the hint. Captain Ford stopped his engine, and the rusty rumrunner lay rolling in the

Pacific swell. Now what? The cutter's captain ordered the *Quadra* to head for San Francisco Bay. Captain Ford refused; he was in international waters and beyond the jurisdiction of the United States vessel. It was no more than a temporary hitch. A boarding party, arms at the ready, swarmed up the side of the *Quadra* and, to no one's surprise, discovered a cargo of rum. So what? A United States vessel still had no business stopping a foreign vessel on the high seas. Precise location is always debatable. But might was right. The *Quadra* was towed into San Francisco. The formal dance was over; face had been saved all round.

Four months after the seizure of the *Quadra*, her captain and crew petitioned United States District Judge George M. Borquin for an immediate trial. Unable to obtain work due to the rumrunning accusations against them and because of their alien status, they claimed to be suffering great hardship. The judge, unhurriedly, took the petition under advisement. Was the situation as bad as the rum ship's men made out? Hardly. The *Quadra's* owners paid the crew full wages throughout the whole dreary wait. It was not an unselfish act; it was on the testimony of the crew that they hoped to get the seizure of the *Quadra* set aside. It would be poor economy to save the wages and lose the ship.

It looked as though the *Quadra's* crew might soon have company. Word came that the *Stadacona* was in trouble, twenty-five miles west of the Golden Gate. The *Quadra* and the *Stadacona* were both rum ships, but there the similarity ended. The *Quadra* was bluff-bowed, rusty and barely seaworthy. The *Stadacona* had class. As the personal yacht of a succession of wealthy industrialists, her clipper bow, low hull lines and raked funnel had been a familiar sight in the fashionable yacht clubs of North America before World War I. Wartime had brought the ship Canadian naval service, renewed peace had brought service as a fisheries patrol vessel, and prohibition had brought work against governments rather than for them. The story goes that when she became a rumrunner her name was changed. Meant to read Mt. Kuyakuz, the ship's nameplate, by inexplicable transposition, eventually read *Kuyakuzmt*. *Kuyakuzmt* it was and so it stayed, possibly in the vain hope that its unpronounceability would confuse the prohibition agencies. It is a good story and possibly true, but if the name was meant to be confusing to American rum chasers, it was likely confusing to many others. When she got into trouble, years after the naming incident, American and Canadian news-papers still referred to her as the *Stadacona*, and no one seemed confused at all.

In early February 1925, bow to the westerly wind, the *Stadacona* pitched with a harsh monotony. With her fuel oil gone, the ship was helpless. By her side rode the coast guard ship *Cahokia*, ordered out to offer help if a storm should threaten danger. But what would be the effect of that help? Would it be a tow to shelter somewhere within the twelve-mile limit? And if help was refused, then what? Might the ship drift inside the twelve-mile limit and be seized? It was an insoluble problem, set by coast guard efficiency. Such was their vigilance, they let it be known, that the supply ships of Rum Row were having trouble off-loading liquor cargoes. Such delays had caused the *Stadacona* to remain off the California coast several weeks longer than her fuel state allowed.

Throughout a long night of wind and rain, the two vessels stayed side by side. The crew of the *Cahokia* stared at the dark shape of the *Stadacona* and waited for help to be requested. It should have been obvious that the rum ship's captain would not have drained his oil tanks without having a plan to fill them again. Far to the north, the *Speedwell*, her decks crammed with lashed-down oil barrels, was sailing to the rescue. It was only a matter of waiting.

The *Speedwell* was destined never to arrive. While the *Stadacona* waited, the oil supply boat burned and stained the sky with a pall of black smoke. Hastily, the schooner *Chief Skugaid* was loaded with oil and sent out on a successful relief voyage. The situation was saved, and within days the *Stadacona* arrived back in Victoria.

The next ship in trouble was the *Coal Harbour*, a wooden, three-masted schooner with auxiliary power. With Captain Charles Hudson in command, the ship was taken by the coast guard cutter *Cahokia* and towed into San Francisco Bay. Describing the incident, Captain Hudson said, "One evening a large U.S. cutter headed straight for us and hailed us to heave to for boarding. I said 'no dice,' and as they tried to come close, we would back off and swing away. This happened on several occasions, but they first got two men aboard us, then seven, and then finally a dozen, who took the tow-line and started us into San Francisco." Captain Johnsen of the *Cahokia* baldly reported that he came alongside after an hour's chase, and left the story of the capture at that. But he did mention a point that Hudson had omitted: at the time of the incident, two nearby boats, seeing the interception, had fled. The implication was that a liquor transfer was either being made or was in the offing. What other reason could there be for a ship loaded with rum and supposedly bound for Champerico, Guatemala to meet close inshore with two boats that should have had no reason to run from the cutter. Close inshore? Hudson claimed that he had been outside territorial limits and had, therefore, been illegally taken while about his business on the high seas. The American authorities were not interested; the seven thousand bottles of liquor found stowed in the holds of the fifty-year-old schooner gave them justification for any slight bending of the rules that might have occurred.

At the beginning of 1925 only the *Quadra* had been lost to the rum trade. By mid-February the *Pescawha* had been escorted into Astoria by the *Algonquin*; the *Stadacona* had been in desperate trouble and had barely escaped; the *Speedwell*, sent to assist the *Stadacona*, had been destroyed by fire; and now the *Coal Harbour* had been towed into San Francisco with Captain Charlie Hudson fuming on the bridge. It was not a good year for Canadian rum-runners. Or for the American drinkers they supplied.

The coast guard had just enjoyed its most effective period on the western ocean, and the booze buyers knew it. A rock-solid law of economics holds that scarcity boosts prices—with no exception provided for illicit drink. A bottle of imported whisky, not long ago selling for $8 a bottle, suddenly cost over $10. And it might get worse, suppliers suggested. Not only had the coast guard put a spoke in the affairs of Rum Row, but the American and Canadian governments were threatening to poke their noses into the private affairs of drinkers.

In the United States there was yet another threat to turn off the tap, which kept a horde of physicians rich and their patients drunk. Once, doctors had supported prohibition. But when it came they were not so sure. Perhaps alcohol was not entirely destructive; perhaps it also had a curative use. Of course, congress could not determine the therapeutic value of alcohol; doctors alone were capable of that. The ultimate end of that argument left doctors free to prescribe alcohol at their discretion. In the first six months of prohibition, fifteen thousand physicians and fifty thousand druggists had applied for licences to prescribe and supply intoxicating liquor. In Chicago alone, half a million prescriptions for whisky were issued within the same period; most of them falsely, the Treasury Department thought. Now, years later, the situation was even worse. Taking the country as a whole, millions of gallons of booze were being prescribed annually. It was too big a loophole to remain open.

North of the border, the end of provincial prohibition had left the British Columbia government as the sole supplier of liquor to the general public. But on the first day that official government liquor stores opened, bootleggers were undercutting government prices. The warehouses in which import/export firms kept their bonded stocks were leaking drink onto the local market. The provincial government, intending to sell at prices determined by monopoly control and its own revenue needs, set out to whip the importers into line. There was a major problem: it was the federal government that regulated imports. Talks were held, and a rumour surfaced that soon the provincial government would become the only legal importer of liquor into British Columbia. The discomfited rumrunners got the picture: if liquor was to be exported from British Columbia, it would have to be purchased through the government liquor board and pass through a customs clearance procedure that would ensure the payment of taxes. Rum trade profits could be expected to drop alarmingly.

In Seattle, Prohibition Director Roy Lyle was jubilant at the news. As he saw it, to make rumrunning pay, liquor would not only have to be smuggled into the United States but also have to be smuggled out of Canada. The effect would be to make liquor smuggling into the United States impossible. Volstead would at last prevail.

Captain Dodge, commandant of the Puget Sound Coast Guard flotilla, agreed with Lyle. The recent successes of the coast guard seemed to have gone to his head. "We have them on the run," said he. "By next summer there won't be a drop of liquor brought direct from British Columbia by water routes." He had the equipment, the men, and the money to make it so. War had been declared. "Shoot-to-kill Orders Given Puget Sound Rum Chasers," "If Runners Fail to Stop, Sink Them," and "Shoot to sink and shoot to kill if they fail to heed stop signals" screamed the headlines of newspapers published on the shores of Puget Sound.

Was rumrunning about to die?

Not according to its main practitioners. Words, and promises of future actions that might never happen, were cheap. A representative of one of Victoria's leading liquor exporters could not believe that U.S. Coast Guard ships would shoot to kill Canadian crews on Canadian vessels. "Think," he said, "what trouble that would bring." He gave no indication that the rumrunning trade would bear any responsibility for possible troubles by its flouting of American prohibition laws. He conceded that small boats operating in the close confines of Puget Sound might be at risk, but large ships carrying the huge quantities of liquor he dealt in always stayed well off the coast in safe waters. As far as he knew, rumrunning was alive and well. A visiting Scottish distiller, rich from supplying the liquor brokers of western Canada with the oceans of liquor they required, put his finger unerringly on the reason for rumrunning's continuation: money. Whatever difficulties were devised by the authorities, there would still be profit to be made. New restrictions would bring new methods of evasion. His main concern was with the use of copies of his product's labels on bottles of inferior liquor, rather than with the demise of west coast rumrunning.

As if to prove that the threats had changed nothing, the *Stadacona*, repaired and with her crew rested after their California adventure, prepared to sail again. The U.S. Coast Guard, having failed to take her when chances had looked so good, had come up with a new strategy. As the *Stadacona* lay at a Victoria dock being loaded with eleven thousand cases of liquor, the coast guard cutter *Snohomish* pulled alongside the same dock and tied up. Theoretically, the *Stadacona*'s cargo, shipped from Canada and cleared for Mexico, was no concern of the United States Coast Guard; practically, such liquor cargoes had an unfortunate habit of being off-loaded onto boats destined for the American shore long before Mexico was reached. The commandant of the Seattle-area coast guard base had a new solution to the problem. Said he, "There is just one thing sure. We are going to trail every big liquor cargo to its destination and see to it that none of the booze is put ashore along our coast. If they clear for Mexico, to Mexico they go."

So when the *Stadacona* put to sea, the *Snohomish* was close behind—as close as three hundred yards: a distance it maintained

U.S.C.G. cutter *Snohomish*, "escort" of the *Stadacona*. *(photo courtesy of the Coast Guard Museum, Seattle)*

in spite of the efforts of the rum ship's captain to shake his "escort." Forsaking the coast, the *Stadacona* turned west and ran for thirty miles before turning south again, quite enough distance from shore to prevent the usual run of small liquor runners from venturing out and loading with contraband liquor destined to slake dry American throats. But still the captain of the *Snohomish* kept his station and left only when relieved by another coast guard cutter opposite the mouth of the Columbia River. The escort service was apparently working well. But the Pacific is a moody

Malahat, queen of the Rum Row supply ships. *(photo courtesy of the Vancouver Maritime Museum)*

ocean. While the visibility remained good, the new escort had no difficulty keeping track of its prey, but as soon as the visibility lessened, contact was lost. When the weather cleared, the *Stadacona*'s radio officer cheerfully reported to base that they were speeding south at twelve knots with not another ship in sight. Once more, Mexico could be forgotten and the California liquor drought relieved.

And there was at least one other ship available to help with the task. Rumour had it that the *Malahat,* recently arrived off the California coast, had a cargo of liquor worth two million dollars for sale: enough to quench a multitude of thirsts. The size of the cargo was rumoured; the presence of the *Malahat* was confirmed by the most reliable of authorities. Captain Lucas of the coast guard cutter *Tamarac* had seen the old schooner and, being too low on fuel to take any other action, had genially waved to the rum ship's crew in passing. The California branch of the coast guard, as overconfident as Captain Dodge on Puget Sound, announced that very little of the *Malahat*'s cargo would ever make it to United States territory. They would see to that. Perhaps they would.

On March 10, 1925, the trial of the *Quadra*'s crew began. The proceedings began slowly. Finding an unbiased jury was difficult. Who, of an age to serve on a jury, had no opinion on prohibition? Who had no leanings at all towards the sides of "wet" or "dry"? Who lacked a relative who held strong opinions one way or the other? Hardly anyone it seemed. The first day was taken up with rejection after rejection of potential jurors. One man had a wife who was a member of a prohibition-supporting organization; he was excused. Another man had made contributions to the Anti-Saloon League; he was dismissed. Yet another man admitted that he had once signed a petition in favour of legalizing light wines and beer and was denied a jury seat. But the acceptance of twelve supposedly good men and true finally came. At least they had one common bond in that each had given a negative answer to the question, "Is the fact that most of the defendants are British subjects likely to cause you to be prejudiced against them?"

The attorneys for the *Quadra*'s owners had no doubt that finding of guilt or innocence would turn on the single point of her geographical position when seized by the coast guard. As their ship was well outside the relatively new twelve-mile limit, the charge must fail. The prosecution agreed that position was important, but as the *Quadra* was taken well inside the set limits, they must win.

What was the position? The answer, obviously, depended on who was asked. The *Shawnee*'s captain, Charles Howell, knew to within a tenth of a mile; both ships were precisely 5.7 miles seaward of the nearest point of the Farallones, an island group thirty miles off San Francisco. Questioned as to his position relative to other landmarks, Captain Howell replied that he had not noticed. The distance travelled by the two ships from the point where the tow began to their berthing position was not known to him, either. He had not wished to have the log come back to haunt him later, and so that source of evidence was lacking. Ensign Morse, the navigating officer of the *Shawnee*, backed up his skipper's testimony. He was certain that the position of interception was as his captain had stated. As they had passed astern of the *Quadra* before coming alongside to put a tow-line on board the rum ship, he had fixed their position using instruments mounted on the cutter's flying bridge. Captain George Ford of the *Quadra* insisted that his ship was at least sixteen miles outside the Farallone Islands when intercepted and seized. The navigating officer was lying: one of Ford's crew had taken a snapshot of the *Shawnee* as she crossed his stern when approaching to tow. An enlargement of the snapshot was entered in evidence. The navigating instruments referred to by Ensign Morse were clearly visible, but Ensign Morse was not to be seen. Had Morse fixed his position when he said or had he not? Two of the *Shawnee*'s crew spoke up in support of the rum-

Rumrunner *Quadra* in her glory days. *(photo courtesy the Seattle Museum of History and Industry ([Seattle Post-Intelligencer Collection])*

runners and said Morse had not fixed a position. Jacob Schybinger swore that no attempt to fix position had been made until the tow had been in progress for an hour and a half. Fred Dobson agreed. But Dobson was an uncertain ally. Since the event, he had been drummed out of the Dry Navy for sleeping on duty—the result of drinking whisky before going on watch. Was he telling the truth or trying to get revenge?

If coast guard men, present or past, could give evidence to aid rumrunners, could rumrunners give evidence to aid the state? They could and did. Was the *Quadra* inside or outside the twelve-mile limit when seized? That was not clear. Was the *Quadra* simply passing down the coast on the way to Mexico or was she engaged in rumrunning? When the next group of witnesses testified, that became crystal clear. Marino Corvelli was a fisherman—sometimes. He had also been an employee of Consolidated Exporters Limited in the past. One of his tasks had been to ferry barrels of whisky from the *Malahat* to the *Quadra*; another to take cargoes of liquor from the *Quadra* to the shore. Salvatori Crivello was equally straightforward in his evidence. "I took eight loads of liquor off the *Malahat*, three off the *Norburn* and one from the *Malahat* and *Quadra* together between April and September last year," he told the court. The evidence was given under a promise of leniency when their own rumrunning exploits were evaluated for punishment. Leniency was fine, but protection was better. Rumrunners had no use for turncoats. Corvelli, Crivello and several other prosecution informants were threatened with death.

At a hotel being used by one informant, a man was stabbed to death—a case of mistaken identity claimed the terrified informant who believed that he was the intended victim.

A bank teller testified that a man had asked him to exchange eighty-two torn one-dollar bills for new bills. Except for the number of bills involved, it was not an uncommon request. But the torn bills had an odd feature; half had lists typed on them. As the lists specified quantities of various kinds of liquor, it took no great imagination to conclude that the mutilated bills had been used in the rum trade. Rum ship captains, it was alleged, tore one-dollar bills in half, kept one half of each and gave the remaining halves to the ship's agent. As customers ashore made arrangements to buy, the agent typed the details of their purchase on one of the half-bills. The customer took the half-bill— an order form with a built-in check on its veracity—and took it to the ship's captain lurking offshore. The captain matched serial numbers of the half-bills presented with those halves he possessed to establish that all was well. The bank teller was unable to recall who had given him the damaged one-dollar bills. But a colleague remembered who had given him similar bills on a previous occasion; it was Vincent Quartararo, alleged local agent of the owners of the *Quadra*. The sum of money involved in the exchanges was trivial; the value of the evidence handed to the prosecution was high. On such penny-pinching acts are cases won and lost.

There were facets of the trial that caused concern. An editorial writer for the Vancouver Sun had words to say on the matter. He had no particular complaint about the normal standard of application of justice in the United States. As far as he could tell, the goddess of justice, blindfolded and with her scales evenly poised, was usually as impartial south of the border as she was anywhere else. But it seemed that there were times when her bandage slipped and revealed an eye. Sometimes the eye winked, and then something that had no business being there was slipped into one or other of her scales. The *Quadra* affair was a case in point. The defendants believed that the ship's position at the time of interception was a vital matter. They were mistaken. Judge John Partridge thought the matter of position irrelevant: he refused to allow the jury to decide whether or not the *Quadra* was within the twelve-mile limit or not. In his view, American ships had the right to seize vessels anywhere on the high seas if conspiracy to break American laws could be proven. Now the scales of justice were really tipped, and the eye of the lady with the scales was winking madly. The editor was perturbed. For a judge to do such a thing was a serious matter. Not only had he interfered with the course of justice, he had also created an unworthy precedent—and that was far more important than the fact that men might be sentenced. For them, the editor had little sympathy; they had been engaged in rumrunning and had been caught. So be it. The judge had at least said something with which the editor heartily agreed: "booze ships are bad places for decent sailor men." But what, asked the editor, would happen if the shoe were on the other foot? How would Americans react if Canadian patrol boats seized American ships on the high seas? Perhaps the howls of protest that emanated from Washington when a poaching American fishing boat was arrested off Canada's Pacific coast gave some idea of the furor that could be expected. The Americans, of all people, should know better than to seize the ships of other nations in international waters. After all, they had fought a war caused in part by British searches of American ships on the high seas—searches, not seizures. The editorial writer demanded that the Canadian government should act to see that Canadian citizens were justly treated, in whatever foreign court they found themselves. In the *Quadra* case, the defensive strategy of the accused had been swept aside by the desire of United States federal officers to secure a conviction and make an example.

With the question of geographical position decided for them, the jury had no difficulty in finding that the various officers and agents of Consolidated Exporters Limited had conspired to breach the prohibition laws of the United States. Sentences were handed out. Charles H. Belanger, a director of Consolidate Exporters was to serve a two-year jail sentence and pay a fine of $10,000, as was Vincent Quartararo, San Francisco agent of the company. Captain George Ford of the *Quadra* was to serve a two-year jail sentence and pay a $1,000 fine. George Harris, first mate, was assessed no fine but sentenced to a prison term of thirteen months. Second Mate Joseph Evelyn drew ten months in the county jail. Chief Engineer J. H. Mason got off relatively lightly with a fine of $500 to be paid for his freedom. The lesser lights of the crew, after being admonished for their poor choice of employment, were ordered deported—including one poor puzzled soul who claimed that he had known the *Quadra* was no longer a Canadian government lighthouse tender when he had signed on but he had not been told that she was a rumrunner. At the time of the trial, the *Quadra* had not been a lighthouse tender for well over a decade.

Three years after the trial ended, the Supreme Court of the United States found no reason to alter the decision of the lower court. The sentences would have to be served and the fines paid. But first the miscreants had to be caught. Captain Ford, it was reported, "is in Canada, a fugitive from justice," and so was everyone else who was wanted. Captain Pamphlet had returned to the United States to serve his sentence after the *Pescawha* incident, but his example was not one that the majority of rumrunners were eager to follow.

The *Quadra* was threatened with a rum ship's ultimate fate. A United States federal court decision allowed the confiscation of cars used by rumrunners about their illicit trade. Good cars, always in short supply, could not be wasted. The confiscated cars were to be added to those already used by customs and prohibition agents. It made good sense to turn the property of rumrunners against them. Cars and ships were both forms of transportation; both carried illicit liquor cargoes. If cars could be confiscated and used to make more effective the application of the country's laws, would it not make sense to use confiscated ships in the same manner?

The *Quadra*, close at hand, was a tempting target for confiscation. The coast guard wanted her for their fleet. The lawyers sharpened their pencils and their wits and went at it. Litigation dragged on interminably. Would the *Quadra* become a member of the Dry Navy, or would she not? The ship supplied the answer. As though exhausted by the ceaseless wrangling about her fate, she sank at her moorings in San Francisco and had to be scrapped. George Winterburn, one-time crew member, was devastated. "She took with her the seven cases of whisky that I had hidden away," he sadly complained.

The *Coal Harbour*'s crew had witnessed the *Quadra* trial with no great joy. Soon it would be their turn to face the court, and undoubtedly the precedent established by Judge Partridge—that distance from the coast was irrelevant when dealing with prohibition offenses—would be used against them. A weak ray of sunshine lit their waiting period. Eight months after their capture, the liquor-laden *Ouiatchouan* was captured outside the Farallone Islands and towed into Sausalito on San Francisco Bay. In spite of the nature of her load, the commander of the area coast guard flotilla failed to press charges. His explanation was that he had no proof that the ship was landing or even planning to land any of her cargo. The *Ouiatchouan* was let go. It was a better-than-expected break in a miserable voyage. The ship, relying on radio transmissions for position fixes, had sailed through thick fog at a speed never exceeding five knots for over three weeks. It was the radio messages that had given her away to the coast guard.

Was this incident, so similar to the taking of the *Coal Harbour*, a sign that she also might be released, or merely further proof of the layman's contention that the law is an ass? That the *Coal Harbour* had been out of the rum trade for eight months was highly satisfactory to United States law enforcement agencies. Any hope that the ship would soon be released to continue her rumrunning career was illusory. When another Canadian rumrunner was towed into San Francisco Bay in 1927, the *Coal Harbour* was still lying at anchor and idle. Legal foot-dragging was as good a way as any to prevent rumrunning ships going about their illicit affairs.

The *Quadra* case had an unexpected sequel. When the trial was over, the prosecuting attorney had words of praise for the crew of the *Shawnee*. To the commandant of the San Francisco coast guard detachment he wrote: "The clean-cut, fine appearance of Captain Charles F. Howell and his men in court, and the straightforward manner in which they testified, has reflected great credit upon the coast guard and the government." But the captain of the cutter turned out to have had more than devotion to duty as his driving force. A rumrunning rival of Consolidated Exporters, keen to reduce competition, had allegedly paid him $20,000 to seize the *Quadra*—inside or outside territorial limits. And another $20,000 had been given to him for lying about the incident in court. Found guilty of perjury, he lost his command. When Captain Charles Hudson later commented, "They were saddled with a rotten law they couldn't enforce," it was difficult to be sure whether he was being critical or understanding. As a seaman with advantages in an unequal struggle, he might well have recognized the frustration that made coast guard officers prey to temptation.

7
THE KING UNTHRONED

Rum dealers occupied a space defined by hazy boundaries. They existed in a world where intelligence was set against counter-intelligence, where loyalties held or were broken, where people kept still tongues or talked, and where promises were kept or ignored as best suited the immediate needs of their makers. Powerful men, on both sides of the prohibition fence, were open to being caught in traps baited with facts gathered by informers. Yet, the statement oversimplifies: some informers, running with the fox and hunting with the hounds, acted as double agents.

The Seattle press liked Roy Olmstead; he was a friendly man, as open as a rumrunner could be, and an endless source of interesting copy. Reporters delighted in describing his acts of impudence as he went about his business under the noses of the local dry agents. He unloaded rum cargoes on the Seattle docks in broad daylight, they told their readers, and carried away the liquor in trucks plastered with signs advertising such innocent contents as meat, fish, bread and vegetables. A huge joke. But an occasional press report showed another side. The *Seattle Times* suggested that Olmstead had corrupted more public officials than anyone in the entire Northwest. To the newspaper, that was immoral; to him, a costly, yet essential business expense. To a police officer proposing payment for a service, the rumrunner com-

Roy Olmstead leaves court with his wife and mother. *(photo courtesy of the Seattle Museum of History and Industry ([Seattle Post-Intelligencer Collection])*

plained that his income was split so many ways that he made nothing. Not so, but the cost was high and had to be met. The greater the number of officials corrupted, the greater was his knowledge of the affairs of the opposition. Unfortunately, the reverse of that coin was that the chances of a double-cross also increased.

In the early twenties a frequent visitor to the offices of the local federal dry agents was a handsome woman named Vivian Potter. The agents considered her a star among their roster of undercover agents. She knew rumrunning well, and her tips had led to liquor caches being found, automobiles carrying illegal booze being seized, and rumrunners being arrested. Naturally, a fair amount of the weight of the law had fallen on the clandestine operations of Roy Olmstead.

But Vivian's successes were trifling matters in the larger scheme of things. She boasted to impressed dry agents that she was about to give a grand jury enough information to affect every rumrunner on the Pacific coast. In fact, when she had finished talking there would be no rum trade left. It was a king-sized boast, but empty. She never visited the dry agents' office again, and for good reason. In late August 1924, Elise Caroline Paiche, alias Elsie Campbell, alias Vivian Potter, married Roy Olmstead, king of west coast rumrunners. Some claim that the story is a myth—one of many that linger from prohibition days. Some claim that the informant who cosied up to the dry squad was not the second Mrs. Olmstead but the first, she who had been divorced by Olmstead days before Elise Caroline Paiche and he had married. It was far from a myth to the newspaper reporter who passed the story on to his readers and included the comment of an irate prohibition official. "Olmstead's marriage to that woman was the wisest thing he ever did—the greatest coup he ever sprang." Perhaps the truth will never be known. But if either wife did the informing, the principle that no one could be trusted had been clearly illustrated.

So Mrs. Elise Caroline Olmstead, usually known as Elsie, moved into the mansion of the rumrunner she had supposedly informed on not long before. Changing sides brought a new set of problems.

Scarcely had she settled into her new home than the Dry Squad came knocking at the door. Everyone in Seattle knew that Roy Olmstead was a rumrunner. A raid at any time in the previous four years would have held out an equal chance of success. Why now? According to cynical observers, it was no more than a public relations ploy. Prohibition Director Roy C. Lyle and his assistant, William M. Whitney were under threat of dismissal on the grounds of ineffectiveness. Here, then, was action to confound the critics. And what action.

The planned raid ran into immediate difficulties. As the prohibition agents were preparing to surround Olmstead's house, a police patrol car turned up. Why, the officers wanted to know, were men standing around in a residential area? What were they up to? When the prohibition agents, obsessed with the need for secrecy, refused to say who they were and what they were doing, the patrolling officers sent them on their way. The Olmstead raid had failed before it had begun.

However, Roy Lyle, having set in motion a scheme designed to save his own neck, was not to be deflected from his purpose. Two days later, free from police interference, the raid was carried out.

The search warrant carried by the prohibition agents as they burst into the Olmstead home had been sworn out on the basis of prohibition agents' observations. One claimed to have heard Elsie Olmstead saying that there was liquor in the house—what he did not say was that having strong drink in the house was not against the law. Many more cars than could be expected to visit a normal home had been seen to arrive and then leave late at night, another agent said. But was that a crime? Hardly. In the last thirty days, agents had seen many people enter the Olmstead house sober and leave intoxicated—but even under prohibition it was not a crime to drink. Yet another agent had heard orders given and taken for the sale of liquor from the house. Now there was an illegality that would justify all as far as the issue of a search warrant was concerned.

As Deputy Director Whitney charged into the house at the head of his agents, he knew what he was looking for. But if he was looking in the right place it seemed that he was not looking at the right time. To his chagrin, there was not a drop of liquor to be found in the house.

When the raid on her home began, Elsie Olmstead knew nothing of it. The woman known as "Aunt Vivian" to her young listeners was reading bedtime stories over the air from the up-stairs broadcasting studio of radio station KFQX, an Olmstead enterprise. Her first clue that all was not well had come when a man burst open the studio door, moved into the room, and stood looking down at her. Indignantly, she had ordered him out. His only reaction had been to tell her not to move. Intimidating Elsie Olmstead was harder than her diminutive size might have suggested. She ignored him and swept out of the room.

Later court testimony given under questioning by Attorney Jerry Finch gave a picture of subsequent events. "You went out?"

"Why, of course. What was to hinder me? I had a right to

leave if I wished. Then I saw Mr. Whitney outside the door. He also told me not to move."

"And what did you do?"

"I went downstairs."

"And then what happened?"

"We didn't trust the agents. So when they went to search the house, my husband suggested that some of the guests accompany each agent."

"Was that done?"

"Yes."

"When was the search finished?"

"About eight or nine o'clock."

"Any liquor found?"

"No."

"When did the agents leave?"

"About 3:30 the next morning."

"About 3:30! What were they doing for so long?"

"Calling up people and telling them to bring liquor."

"Did these agents represent themselves to be some person else when they called up these people?"

"Yes. Mr. Whitney said he was a man named Fletcher. Mrs. Whitney said she was I. I heard some of the other agents say, 'Yes, this is Roy.' Once I tried to use the telephone, but Whitney struck me in the face, pushed me against the wall, and took it from me."

Legalities and boorish behavior aside, the Olmstead rumrunning organization had suffered a blow. The dry agents found that three of the sixteen guests present had no right to be working in the United States. Lawmen and rumrunners all too often seemed to have had an overwhelming desire to be on the same side. Two of the aliens had been members of the Canadian Northwest Mounted Police. Olmstead employed one as a book-keeper and the other as his superintendent of transportation. The last of the alien trio, another bookkeeper, had no police connection—other than the one causing him current embarrassment. Freed on bail the day after the raid, all three disappeared over the Canadian border.

The prohibition service was working hard to pin whatever unpleasant label they could devise on anyone involved with Roy Olmstead. Remarkably, they who had used Vivian Potter as a trusted informant not long before, alleged that the same woman, now known as Elsie Olmstead, was probably an illegal immigrant.

William Whitney, raider of the Olmstead mansion. *(photo courtesy of the Seattle Museum of History and Industry ([Seattle Post-Intelligencer Collection])*

Her claim of legal entry into the United States in 1920 could not be substantiated from immigration records. In addition, she was accused of being a bigamist; an informant had told of her abandoning a husband and family in Canada before moving south. And her activities as a radio announcer were suspected of having a seamy side; the stories she read were coded messages aimed at rumrunners rather than at children. True or not, the prohibition officers tried to close the station by having a parts supplier attach all the Olmstead's radio equipment for an outstanding bill of only $139.75.

Whitney and his men had managed to collect a few bottles of booze before they had eventually trooped out of the Olmstead mansion early in the morning. Phillip Karenski, an Olmstead distributor, had turned up at an unfortunate time clutching three bottles to his chest. Carl Wilson, Hobart Hector, Isadore Fischler and Meyer Rose had also brought bottles. All were Olmstead retailers; all had been invited by the prohibition agents' telephone calls to join the party and bring a few bottles. The bottles would not help prove that the Olmsteads had liquor for sale in their home. Syd Green, first lieutenant of Olmstead's organization, had turned up in his new car during the raid. Agents who had expected him to surrender leapt for their lives as he stepped on the gas and roared off into the night.

As the Olmstead raid was taking place, Clarence G. "Baldy" Healy, another Olmstead operator, was being arrested. Why, was not clear. The agents had expected his home to contain a cache of liquor. It did not. Putting the best possible face on their failure, the agents claimed to have found evidence that liquor had recently been removed. The lack of liquor in homes where it was almost certain to be found for sale any day in the year was puzzling. Perhaps Olmstead's business expenses for informers had shown a return.

But all this was skirmishing. It would be a long time before the courts got down to cases. A mass of business papers relating to rumrunning had been removed from the Olmstead household, and its analysis would take weeks. If weeks were available. The warrant authorizing entry into Olmstead's home had specified a search for liquor, no more. According to Jerry Finch, Roy Olmstead's lawyer, the papers had been removed illegally and must be returned without delay.

A small cloud appeared on the horizon. In discussing the raid, Lyle took pains to discount a rumour that wire-taps had been used to gather evidence. Jerry Finch knew better; he claimed that the dry side had wire-tap reports making up a volume fifteen inches thick. It was a cloud that would grow until it blotted out the topic of rumrunning, which was supposedly the core of the case.

For Roy Olmstead it was business as usual. Many Seattle residents depended upon him for employment. More depended on him for liquor supplies. Rumrunning would not stop because his house had been raided. He was not a criminal until so proven. Life must go on. Thanksgiving Day, 1925, brought more grief. As Olmstead and his men were unloading the cargo of a speedboat and transferring it to parked automobiles, prohibition agents moved in and arrested them. Evidence was not lacking; scattered around were burlap-wrapped bottles containing 1,332 quarts of smuggled liquor. Said Olmstead, hands in air as he faced the guns, "It looks like things are going very bad for Olmstead." Arrested with him was Alfred Hubbard, a trusted henchman, out on bail for a rumrunning incident that had happened a few days before. Rumrunning was a tangled web, and somewhere in that web was a strand that possibly led back to an informer who had betrayed Olmstead.

In January 1926, a few days after "Cannonball" Baker and Harry Sowash had been hanged in Vancouver's Oakalla jail for the murder of Captain William Gillis and his son, a federal grand jury in Seattle indicted ninety persons for conspiring to violate the prohibition laws of the United States and to evade the payment of tariffs. Of the ninety named, thirty-two, including Roy Olmstead, his wife, two police officers, an attorney, a customs broker, an inventor, and a further mixed bag of Olmstead employees, were arrested and then released when bail bonds were posted. It was not a laughing matter: the maximum penalty for both conspiracy and tariff evasion was two years hard labour with the imposition of a heavy fine as additional punishment. When the trial began, the main courtroom protagonists were District Attorney Thomas P. Revelle on one side and Jerry Finch and George F. Vanderveer on the other. Although acting for Roy Olmstead, Finch had been dumped by some of the rumrunner's men; they had chosen instead to be represented by George Vanderveer, a rough, tough, brawling attorney known as "the counsel for the damned," in the belief that he would be a more likely saviour.

Jerry Finch was a persuasive man, and one not averse to gilding the lily. Speaking of Roy Olmstead, he painted a picture of a devoted patron of the arts and sciences and a solid man of business. Had Olmstead not started the first radio station in Seattle? Did he not employ a scientist to work on improving that radio station so that culture and the arts could be more widely enjoyed? Many residents of Seattle must have been astonished to hear that their favourite liquor supplier was such a man of culture. The "solid man of business" was much easier to envisage: rumrunning was a business, and a field of endeavour in which Olmstead was second to none. Finch admitted that his client had been linked to rumrunning—by mistake. Once Mr. Olmstead had held an interest in Western Freighters, the Canadian owners of the *Prince Albert*. His understanding had been that the ship was engaged in the legitimate business of transporting liquor from Vancouver, British Columbia, to Ensenada, Mexico. As soon as he had realized his mistake, he had withdrawn from the business.

But the prosecution knew there was more to it than that and

turned Roy Olmstead's own words against him to prove it. District Attorney Thomas Revelle had the transcripts of many of Olmstead's recent telephone calls, wire-taps that Prohibition Director Lyle had once insisted had never been made. And, in addition, the prosecution had on hand business documents seized in the raid on the Olmstead home and those later taken from the offices of Jerry Finch. The evidence contained made it clear that a conspiracy to violate the prohibition laws and evade tariffs had existed.

Interestingly, Roy Olmstead knew that his phones were tapped. He had been approached by Richard Fryant, who had shown him transcripts of conversations regarding liquor deals made on Olmstead's office phone. Fryant had a deal to make; he would sell Olmstead the transcripts for $10,000. Fryant was invited to go to hell. Roy Olmstead knew about the laws of evidence; wire-tapping was against the law. The knowledge that his phones were tapped gave the rum boss a means of leading prohibition agents astray. Often he gave false information over his home phone about planned liquor landings and then went to a public phone and issued different instructions. As a result, agents often set up an ambush in one place while illicit cargoes came peacefully ashore many miles away. On one famous occasion, prohibition agents had been decoyed to a lonely shore, and while they had watched in vain for a liquor landing, a lighted lantern had been hung in one of their cars. It was a mockery that invited revenge. Trying to catch Roy Olmstead smuggling by listening to his telephone conversations had brought the prohibition agents nothing but grief. But now they were laughing. It was not necessary to catch him red-handed; the charge against him was conspiracy to violate prohibition laws, not their actual violation. For that, the misleading telephone calls were as valuable as any. Roy Olmstead had obligingly put his neck in a noose.

The way out for the defense was to get the documentary and wire-tap evidence ruled inadmissible. Attorney Jerry Finch, defendant as well as defender, claimed that the removal of the documents from his office and the Olmstead household was unconstitutional. Judge Neterer disagreed, and ruled that the documents were admissible evidence. His view counted. George Vanderveer, enraged at not being permitted to see the transcripts of the wire-taps—while the prosecution side made frequent reference to them—concentrated on getting them banned from the courtroom. His arguments, both legal and moral failed.

But something of importance had occurred; the trial now had a larger, more important dimension and was becoming known as the "Whispering Wires Case."

The trial was a long, drawn-out affair with evidence and argument lasting for over a month. A hard time for men with a probable jail sentence in their immediate future. Yet Roy Olmstead, the man likely to get the longest sentence of all, showed no outward concern. Day after day, he appeared in court, affable, smooth, urbane. Possibly his lack of concern was a pose masking inner turmoil. On his way to court one morning, his car and another met in a grinding collision. His actions, for a man known for his pleasant manner and unaggressive style, were unexpected. Leaping from his car, he swung a wicked uppercut in the direction of the other driver's jaw—and missed. He swung again, this time with his foot, and connected with the other man's groin. His opponent swung and landed a blow on Olmstead's chin. They grappled, fell to the ground, and, after being pried apart, went their separate ways, each blaming the other for the accident. It was, according to a wry comment in a local newspaper, a fistic battle in which the Marquis of Queensbury rules were ignored.

When the lawyers on both sides had had their say, Judge Jeremiah Neterer instructed the jury. He had allowed wire-tap evidence; the rights and wrongs of that decision were not for its consideration. The task of a jury was to uphold the law so that anarchy should not prevail. Fairness was essential. The jury must see that no innocent person was convicted and no guilty person allowed to escape. Guilty or innocent? The judge had no doubts. "My opinion," he said, "is that a conspiracy has been established between Olmstead and some of the defendants on both counts. But you are not to take this opinion into consideration." Once said, how could it be ignored?

The jury began deliberating at nine in the morning. With a list of defendants of such length it was not expected that they would return a verdict soon. An hour passed. Two hours. Lunchtime came and went. There was an uneasy edge to the waiting crowd. An observer, reaching for effect, described the scene: "The courtroom was a shadowy study in gloom as the word got round that the jury was coming in and the benches began to fill. Nervous men, roughly dressed, with bloodshot eyes, slumping into their seats. Wives and daughters and mothers, solid rows of them. Florid hats, matador red, cathedral blue, mignonette, shading faces boldly lined, yellow with anxiety, beneath defiant dabs of rouge."

The wife of a defendant scribbled her prediction of the verdict—or was it her hope of what might be?—and passed it to others to cheer them up. Lawyer Jerry Finch made a weak joke about the rent he owed on his office. Roy Olmstead, sitting beside his wife, looked much paler than usual. Why was it all taking so long? The jury shuffled in and took their seats in the jury box. Rollin Sandford, a Seattle banker, occupied the first seat, an indication that he had been elected jury foreman. Judge Neterer spoke, "Gentlemen, have you reached your verdict?" Sandford replied with a single word, "Yes." He rose and handed the judge an envelope. With maddening deliberation, the judge opened the envelope, took out several sheets of paper and carefully read each to himself. No shadow of expression crossed his face. When he was fully informed, the judge handed the sheets of paper to the clerk of the court. Now for it. The clerk started to read and, one by one, the majority of the accused men heard themselves judged guilty. But not all were found guilty: seven men were to be freed immediately, as was Elsie Olmstead. Elsie was caught between sadness and joy; sadness that others, including her husband, had been found guilty, but joyful at her own escape. She moved from group to group, offering sympathy and support, but it was perhaps a measure of her steely backbone that of all the women in the courtroom she alone was reported to "have kept her powder dry."

Sentencing was delayed one week and bail set to ensure attendance. Men with wives and children to support had their bail amounts set at modest sums. But the judge's concern with family welfare was not universal. To Roy Olmstead he said shortly, "Let the new bond be the same as the old."

Olmstead replied, "I have always thought that the old one was exorbitant."

"No, I think not," was the judge's response. "It will remain the same—$10,000."

"I've got a wife and family," Olmstead persisted, "and I won't run away."

Not by the flicker of an eye did Judge Neterer indicate that there was any hope of a change of heart.

Olmstead capitulated. "Well, I thank your Honour, just the same."

Such were the perils of leadership in the rumrunning trade.

It was a serious business, but there was a ray of humour associated with the trial. W.G. Beardslee, a rising young lawyer, offered his services at no charge so that he could participate in what he saw as an important legal event. His offer was accepted but the cost to him was more than time and effort—he also lost $100. Defendant Clyde Thompson, unable to afford a lawyer, was assigned to Beardslee. The lawyer boasted in public that he would get his client off and was willing to make a $100 bet on it.

"Shucks," commented a young man nearby, "you don't know this fellow Thompson; he's a no-good bum. I'll take the bet." Lawyer Beardslee, delighted to get a taker, fished for the taker's name. "I don't believe we've met," he said.

"No," was the reply. "We haven't. I'm Clyde Thompson."

Beardslee, in the belief that he already knew as much of the case as he needed to know, had not taken the trouble to contact his client. As it turned out, Thompson won the $100: a welcome contribution in helping pay the fine imposed when he was found guilty.

When sentencing occurred, Roy Olmstead was given four years in jail, two years on each count, fined $8,000 and given a lecture for good measure. More in sorrow than in anger, Judge Neterer spoke of what was and what might have been, "If the same energy and organization had been directed along legitimate lines, with lawful purposes, great good might have been obtained. If you do not realize now that you have grievously erred, then I feel sorry for you."

Olmstead seemed unimpressed. His comment to reporters was that he still considered buying and selling whisky to be no crime. He would take a gambler's chance and try an appeal. Not that it would do much good. Judges stuck together and upheld each other.

Immediately the case ended, the Olmstead residence, magnificently furnished and set in beautiful grounds, was advertised for sale—a steal at $35,000. Why was the house being sold? prying reporters wanted to know. Was it to raise money to pay legal expenses? Roy Olmstead gave a terse reply. "For more than four weeks I have been sitting in a courtroom listening to this person and that tell a judge and jury what my motives were for doing things. I am selling my house. Why I am selling it is something I shall keep to myself. I have decided to tell nothing."

In October 1927, the rest of the ninety people indicted were tried. The star witness was Alfred M. Hubbard, one of Olmstead's trusted lieutenants in the rumrunning business. When Olmstead was caught red-handed on Thanksgiving Day, 1925, Hubbard was present. But that was no proof of his loyalty. Two months before the capture, Hubbard had secretly joined the other side and Roy Lyle had written a gloating letter to Washington, predicting the imminent downfall of Olmstead and those in government service who protected his interests. When, well after the fact of defection, Jerry Finch heard of it, he burst into tears. Olmstead was calmer. He expected disloyalty; that was the nature of the business.

In his evidence, Alfred Hubbard did three things. First he gave the public a brief lesson on rumrunning terminology and business practices. As far as the thirsty man-in-the-street knew, you wanted a bottle of booze and there was a friendly local supplier round the corner ready to oblige. There was no reason to fret over where he got it from and how. Cost was important, though. Prices varied. Hubbard explained why. When landing liquor, it was possible to "shoot it" or "let it ride." Shooting it called for payment in advance. There was an advantage—that of lower price. But there was also a disadvantage—that of greater risk. An intercepted cargo meant a complete loss. Letting it ride called for payment on delivery, which lessened the risk for the middle man but cost him more as a result. Secondly, Hubbard tied most of the alleged rumrunners to specific liquor transactions. Memory seemed not to be a problem as he named names, identified places and specified times. But if his memory was clear, his voice was not; often it shook as he caught the malevolent stares of his one-time cronies. Thirdly, he went for those supposedly in opposition to the rumrunners. Roy Olmstead, Hubbard claimed, was able to pass his rum-laden boats through the waters of Puget Sound with impunity for the simple reason that many of the men set to catch him were in his pay. It was no small deal; the rot was deep-rooted. When prohibition service agents and police officers failed to see Olmstead's illicit cargoes passing it, was due to a blindness brought on by orders from above. How high did it go? As high as recently retired Captain Dodge, formerly in command of the Northwest division of the United States Coast Guard, claimed Hubbard—and beyond that to William M. Whitney, assistant director of the federal prohibition office in Seattle. It was a messy trial, full of deceit, intrigue and lies. The rum trade was more complex than the image presented to the world by the dapper and affluent Roy Olmstead. There was a seamier side. The accused were the men who did the deeds that others sometimes chose to glamourize. Men who routinely broke the law, unpopular though that law might be; men determined to save their own skins at any cost. But the tactics of the prosecution were no better than those of the defendants. The prosecution had used questionable methods in the first Olmstead trial and, apparently, saw no reason to change. By the time the trial was over, the waters had been thoroughly muddied.

When the time came for the jury to clear the muddy waters, there were thirty-six individual verdicts to be made. Fourteen men with names that had been bywords in the liquor traffic of Puget Sound for several years were found guilty. Twenty-two of the accused were found not guilty and freed. Hubbard's evidence, good enough to convict his former rumrunning colleagues, was judged insufficient to convict the public officials said to be in the pay of rumrunners; all were freed.

Alfred Hubbard quickly found that working on both sides had dangers. To say that he was not popular is to seriously understate the case. Outside the courtroom after the sentences had been handed out, he was hit in the face by Mrs. Benjamin Goldsmith, wife of one of those sentenced. Hubbard slapped her with the nearest weapon to hand—his hat. Mrs. Goldsmith's husband and another man stepped in. One struck Hubbard and others rushed into the fray. Hubbard retreated, followed by an angry crowd. It was then that William M. Whitney, assistant prohibition director, went for his gun and threatened to fire into the crowd if they didn't back off. Hubbard, seizing his chance, escaped.

It was an incident of low comedy marking a turning point in Washington State rumrunning. After two court cases, Olmstead's organization lay in ruins while he awaited the outcome of the various appeal opportunities open to him. The rumrunning business would never be the same, but it was still going on as was shown by a newspaper report from Bellingham. There, as the Olmstead trial results were being announced, a car containing twenty-three cases of liquor had been stopped. As the Canadian border was only a handful of miles to the north, the liquor's point of origin was obvious. The car had not been stopped without incident. On being flagged down by the police, the driver, Edward Smith, had stamped down hard on the accelerator. He stopped when a bullet shattered his foot. The shot that got him must have been the world's greatest fluke; after hitting Smith's foot the bullet passed on and neatly removed both heels from the shoes of Lillian Murphy, who was sitting beside him. She, in a car containing twenty-three cases of liquor, denied all knowledge of its existence—she had only gone along for the ride. A second car, following on behind, stopped on command. Twenty-nine more cases of liquor were found. The sentencing of the Seattle rumrunners was not a general discouragement; their removal would simply create greater opportunities for others.

Olmstead's pessimism about his chances of acquittal on appeal seemed justified. He had been found guilty, jailed and freed on bail. But he was far from free; the watching went on. At one point, A.V. Williams, a surety for Olmstead's bail bond, asked to withdraw as bondsman. Alarm bells rang. Where was Roy Olmstead? The authorities soon knew. A tapped telephone call from Canada had requested Elsie Olmstead to call her husband at a number in Victoria, British Columbia. What was a man on bail doing out of the country? Why did Williams want to withdraw as bondsman? To the lawmen there was only one possible answer: Roy Olmstead was preparing to leave the jurisdiction of the United States and become a resident of Canada. Olmstead was amused. "I couldn't if I wanted to," he declared. "They wouldn't let me in." The lawmen, unimpressed by his statement, put him in the county jail on his return.

At the end of November 1927, Roy Olmstead had reason, well based or not, to argue that his prediction of judges sticking together was correct. The circuit court of appeals in San Francisco found no reason to reverse the lower court decision to punish him. The defense claim that the use of wire-tap evidence violated both the seizure clause of the Fourth Amendment to the constitution and the self-incrimination clause of the Fifth Amendment was rejected. But one judge dissented. Judge Frank Rudkin noted that a book containing wire-tap transcripts had been used by the prosecution. It seemed to Judge Rudkin that each time the book was used "the book not the witness was speaking." Many intercepted phone messages had been transcribed. Fairly? Accurately? Who could tell? It was clear that all sorts of possibilities for error existed and, in addition, all sorts of opportunities for planting evidence. Judge Rudkin believed that "a better opportunity to colour or fabricate testimony could not well be devised by the wit of man." It was not good enough. He also had grave reservations on the morality of wire-tapping.

Roy Olmstead went to jail, but Judge Rudkin's dissent had given him hope that the Supreme Court might see things his way.

After some dithering, the Supreme Court decided to look into the wire-tap aspect of the case alone and arrived at a majority decision that wire-tapping was not illegal. In the view of the chief justice, a person who installed a telephone with connecting wires intended to project his voice outside the house. That being so, it was reasonable that those outside should hear. Undoubtedly, there was a moral aspect, but that was overridden by the need to protect the public from unlawful acts. It was not in the interest of society to set such high standards of evidence gathering that criminals would benefit. But the majority was narrow. Five powerful judges dissented, and the tenor of their objection was that Americans had a constitutional right to privacy that governments could not unjustifiably breach — and that included a right to privacy on the telephone. If governments that applied the law failed to maintain the constitutional rights of citizens, they would, themselves, become lawbreakers, contempt for the law would flourish and anarchy would result. From a tawdry rumrunning case had emerged a powerful statement on civil liberties.

For Roy Olmstead the future was clear. His avenues of appeal were exhausted, and his sentence must be served. And served it was. After thirty-five months in McNeill Island Prison, he was released. But in that time, Olmstead had undergone a remarkable transformation. Rumrunning still existed but returning to it was no longer an option he cared to choose. On release he told newsmen that McNeill Island Prison had seen the last of him. Time would prove him wrong. Soon he was back as a Christian Scientist convert working among the prisoners. The old Roy Olmstead was no more.

In 1935 his changed character brought a presidential pardon for his past misdeeds.

8
UNDER THE GUNS

The rum ship had been taken by force and towed into port. Proceedings for the vessel's confiscation were under way. It seemed to be the old familiar story, but there was a difference. The United States Coast Guard, encouraged by previous successes, had reached a level of aggressiveness that was about to bring a harsh rebuke.

After listening to both sides, Judge George M. Borquin, bluntly stated his opinion. The seizure of the *Federalship* had been illegal. How could it have been otherwise when the ship had been taken by the use of arms in international waters? Reaching back more than a hundred years for an apt illustration, the judge pointed out that such naked trespass and aggression on the high seas had been a cause of the war of 1812. His voice dripped acid. Surely some progress had been made in the relations between countries during the past century. Were not treaties in force to regulate the conduct of nations? Did not harmonious relations and the avoidance of war require that those treaties be held inviolate? Clearly, the United States Coast Guard had transgressed. In effect, the overeager coast guard had tripped on its own determination to put an early end to the career of a new rum ship on the coast. The *Federalship*, formerly the *Gertrude* of Belgium, newly arrived in Vancouver, had taken on board eleven thousand cases of liquor in transit from Glasgow to South America. There was nothing furtive about the loading. Anyone with eyes could see the cases of liquor disappearing into the ship's hold, and that included American prohibition agency spies who sniffed in disbelief when told of the intended destination. They knew all about shipments from Canada to South America—and to Mexico—and to all the other fanciful destinations dreamed up by rumrunners. When the ship left port on February 22, 1927, its departure was immediately reported to prohibition agency headquarters in Washington.

The *Federalship* ducked round the southern tip of Vancouver Island and set out into the Pacific Ocean. Along her route, she picked up as a shadow the coast guard cutter *Algonquin*. That was not an immediate problem; there would be plenty of time for evasion later. But the captain of the *Federalship* might have been less relaxed about the situation had he known that the *Algonquin*'s captain had orders that went far beyond acting as a passive escort.

After days of steaming, the *Federalship* was ordered to heave-to. Captain Stone, glaring from his bridge, refused to obey. A warning shot was fired. Stone ignored it, but the odds against him were lengthening. Three other coast guard cutters appeared from over the horizon and soon four armed ships were circling the merchantman. The warning shot had not slowed the rumrunner by a single knot. Coast guard orders covered such an eventuality. Deliberate aim was taken at the recalcitrant skipper's steering gear. Deliberate but inaccurate. The roar of the cannon was closely followed by a hatch cover on the *Federalship*'s deck splintering into jagged shards. This was war. And a very one-sided war. The hatch cover had not been far from the ship's bridge. Captain Stone stopped his ship, and it lay rolling in the Pacific swells. The nearest land lay three hundred miles away. On the supposedly free high seas, a Canadian-owned ship, crewed by Canadian officers and seamen, outward bound for South America, had been fired on and damaged by ships owned by the United States government. It was a blatant act of aggression, protested Captain Stone, but his protest was ignored. The *Federalship* was towed into San Francisco Bay with a prize crew in control.

There was an odd twist in the situation. Canadian owners and crew would normally have been under the protection of

Great Britain, but not this time. Bought in Belgium, the *Federalship* had passed directly from Belgian to Panamanian registry. The coast guard strategists who had ordered her capture had approved the use of force only if the Panamanian flag was being flown. As expected, it was.

Why should it make a difference what flag the ship was flying when three hundred miles from land? The government high-ups in Washington, D.C., had their own peculiar point of view on that. Twisting the tail of the British lion on naval matters was unwise; flicking a little salt water into the face of Panama would bring no retribution.

The official attitude was based on pragmatism; the attitude of Judge Borquin on fairness and law. He ordered ship and crew released. Releasing the crew was simple; getting the ship back more difficult. There were bureaucratic wires to be uncrossed. Many wires. Enough wires to build a cage. The presence nearby of the *Coal Harbour*, in her third year of captivity, should have made that clear. Delay was a very important tool in the rum war. Ships tied up in United States ports carried no rum.

As the American authorities saw it, the country of registry of the *Federalship* was a joke. The ship was Canadian-owned, manned by a Canadian crew and was carrying a million dollar liquor cargo. It was, in short, a Canadian rumrunner. The authorities were weary of having rumrunners hide behind legal trickery. When Captain Stone and two attorneys employed by his company demanded the release of the Federalship, the official they faced was willing to discuss the weather, but not the ship's release. The owners' legal representatives took the matter back to court. Judge Frank Kerrigan, set the task of giving a definitive answer to the ship's fate, ordered her turned her loose. Now two judges had ruled for release.

Captain Stone saw an opportunity to make the coast guard look foolish. He insisted that when the *Federalship* steamed out of San Francisco it must be with an escort of coast guard cutters—just as she had steamed in. And the escort must accompany him to the exact position where they had illegally detained his ship. They had forced him to sail three hundred miles in; he would force them to sail three hundred miles out. From that position he would resume his voyage to South America.

He would have to wait awhile to enjoy his triumph. The

words of the second judge had no more immediate effect than had those of the first. Several government departments must have their requirements met before the *Federalship* could sail.

The crew members were spitting nails as time dragged on and conflicting stories ebbed and flowed like ocean tides. They were leaving. They were not leaving. Soon they would sail. Permission to sail had been denied—again. The lawyers beavered away until it seemed that the last wire of the restraining cage had been cut away. The Secretary of the Treasury's department came to the end of its objections. The Attorney General's department had no further objections to the ship's release. And, finally, the Secretary of State's department withdrew its objections. Now freedom for the *Federalship* depended on a mere lieutenant of the coast guard. He balked. Lieutenant Austin complained that he had not been given a direct order to free the *Federalship*. Until he had such an order, she would stay where she was. A special order quickly solved the problem. The balky lieutenant assigned men to assist the *Federalship*'s crew to make the whisky-laden ship ready for her voyage. The vessel would be released in a condition as good as when it was seized; allowing for normal wear and tear, added Austin cautiously. Down in the grimy stokehold of the *Federalship*, shovels flashed as coal was hurled into open firebox grates. For the first time in weeks, the pressure gauges showed a healthy head of steam. The sweating stokers had never worked so happily. Soon they would be at sea.

But, no sooner had Lieutenant Austin delivered his message than the release order was countermanded. No one knew why. Washington had spoken, that reason was enough. Inexplicably, the order was withdrawn within hours. The ship was free to go—again.

It was too much to believe. By many it wasn't believed; they expected the ship to be detained again at the last moment. It was not to be. As Captain Stone sailed his ship under the Golden Gate Bridge, his grin was almost as wide as the Pacific Ocean that lay ahead. In his pocket he had a small present for the owners; $413, courtesy of the United States government, in payment for ship's supplies seized and sold on arrival in port.

The *Federalship* got its escort, but it was not the armada originally envisioned by Captain Stone. And to no one's surprise, he headed for Vancouver instead of South America. As far as the Columbia River, the coast guard cutter *Shawnee* stayed close. From the Columbia River mouth to within sight of the ship's destination, the *Algonquin* danced attendance. But the escort was not so much an act of contrition on the part of the United States government as a means of keeping the *Federalship*'s cargo from leaking onto United States shores. In a way, it was too late. On arrival in Vancouver, the ship's owners insisted that 2,000 cases of liquor had been stolen while the ship was in the hands of the United States government. That was a loss to be considered when damages were set. Another consideration for the owners was the ship's Panamanian registry. What use had that been to them? Dockside gossip suggested that another change of registration was due.

The alcoholic drought brought about by the capture of the *Federalship* was brief. Three rumrunning attempts scotched in a single night suggested that somewhere off the California coast a new menace to sobriety was open for business.

Twenty miles south of San Francisco, carefully concealed among coastal sand-dunes, a group of prohibition agents kept watch. Through night-glasses, they could see a small boat, her bow grounded in sand, being unloaded. Tension among the agents was high. Men pulled at collars suddenly grown too tight. Sand worked into awkward places and made them squirm. Holster flaps were opened and revolvers checked for ease of drawing. Then the quiet burble of a boat's engine running at low power started, faded in the distance, and died. The rumrunning boat was gone, and on the coast road vehicles were being loaded unhurriedly, as though there was all the time in the world to get the job done. But time was more limited than it seemed. Just before the convoy was ready to move off, the agents advanced with weapons drawn. Five of the rumrunners who had gone for their guns threw them down and hoisted their hands high. A sixth man ran, ducking and weaving among a hail of poorly aimed bullets, and escaped. The agents had done well: nine hundred cases of liquor had been seized and five captured men were handcuffed and helpless. Among them was Joe Parente, a notorious rumrunner who was out on bail while appealing a sentence given for a previous incident.

Predictably, Parente had an explanation for his evening's activities. He insisted that he had not been rumrunning that night. The prohibition agents found that hard to swallow. What had he been doing, they asked? Why, he said with an air of injured innocence, he and his friends had been out along the coast road enjoying the night air when they had come across a group of men loading a truck. For some reason, the men had run off. Just as he and his friends were innocently looking over the truck to see what was going on, the agents had arrived and almost scared them to death.

While Joe Parente was trying to convince the prohibition agents of the truth of his unlikely story, another smuggling disaster was taking place not far away. The fast speedboat *A-287*, heading in from the open ocean with a load of liquor, was fired on by the coast guard cutter *Gaviota*. Immediately, the throttles were rammed open and the bow wave of the rumrunning boat creamed higher. Orders to stop were ignored. Unwilling to be ignored, the rum chaser's crew pumped out a hail of rifle fire that peppered the sea around the fleeing speedboat. Cut off to seaward, the only way to go was straight for the shore. Choosing a grounding in preference to capture, the rumrunners drove their vessel onto the beach near Santa Cruz. Boat and cargo were lost. And so, in a sense, were the crew. As the speedboat slithered to a halt in a lather of sand and foam, they leapt into the water, waded ashore, and escaped among the sand dunes. It was ironic that the rum chaser *Gaviota* was a converted rumrunner.

Twenty miles north of San Francisco, on the verge of seizing an illicit cargo of liquor, a pursuing rum chaser developed engine trouble and lost its quarry. One thousand cases of liquor had eluded their grasp, the authorities said. How was the size of the unseen cargo known? How had the authorities been able take action at three widely scattered liquor landing locations in one night—right places, right times? Perhaps rumrunners were their own worst enemies. They lived in a fiercely competitive world, and the night's events eased the strain for those untouched. Perhaps a pointed hint or two to the enforcement agencies had brought about the desired decrease in competition.

If a Tahitian visitor was to be believed, the liquor in the aborted landings had come from the Canadian supply ship *Malahat*. When he had left home, talk around the port of Papeete had suggested that the enormous liquor cargo on the ship was intended to ease the dry throats of Californians. It was the kind of rumour that coast guard officers could believe, and all the more easily when San Francisco was once more awash with every type of liquor that could be'desired.

The sailing of the *Malahat* from Tahiti marked a new twist in the rum trade. Canada, pressed by the United States, had started to make life difficult for rumrunners. A commission had been set the task of discovering whether ships leaving Canadian ports landed their duty-free liquor cargoes at their declared destinations or had them smuggled into the United States. Judging by the landing certificates turned in by ship owners, all was well. Judging by the evidence given before the commission, all was far from well.

In his evidence, the chief customs collector for the port of Victoria named names. The *Prince Albert, Stadacona* and *Lirio de Agua* often cleared for Central America ports and invariably supplied certificates of unloading as proof of compliance. But were the certificates believable? He thought not. Why would liquor sent in bond from Scotland pass through the Panama Canal, traverse the length of Central America's Pacific shore, sail the entire length of California, Oregon and Washington, be landed in British Columbia, and then be sent back to a port in Central America that had been a stone's throw from the outward track? Recently, the *Eva B* had been seized and sold when found carrying cases of liquor which had been a part of the cargo of the *Prince Albert* when cleared for a distant foreign port. As he spoke, the *Lirio de Agua*, supposedly bound for Nicaragua, was under seizure for transferring a thousand cases of liquor to a Vancouver coastwise boat. And how could the *Quadra* have had most of her liquor cargo still in her holds when seized by the United States Coast Guard? Before the seizure had occurred, a document testifying to the unloading of that cargo in San Salvador had already arrived in British Columbia. How could it be that a small boat had declared its destination to be Mexico three times, provided landing certificates for all three trips, and taken only fifty-six hours to accomplish the feat?

Captain Fred Billington, one-trip skipper of the *Stadacona* told how he had taken on 7,040 cases of liquor, some of which came from a Vancouver bonded warehouse, some from a similar warehouse in Victoria, and some manufactured in Canada by Hiram Walker & Sons of Windsor, Ontario. The cargo had been cleared for Buena Ventura, Columbia. The ship's owners had given Billington rather different orders, and he had, in fact, held

a position twenty miles off San Francisco for fifty-two days during which time he had off-loaded his entire cargo to speedboats
that had landed it on the California coast. The papers certifying
that he had unloaded his cargo in a port that he had never seen
were not a problem. They were handed to him by the captain of
one of the small pick-up boats. Captain Billington had only
done this once; a thirty-four-year veteran of the sea, he had not
found rumrunning to his taste.

A former captain of the *Jessie*, claiming to be a law-abiding
man, explained that he was not one of those shipmasters who
cleared for South American ports and then dropped off his
cargo en route. Not he! Invariably, he set out to sea in ballast,
but carrying sufficient stores for a long voyage, and opened his
employer's sealed instructions when three days out. His orders
specified positions at sea where he was to meet other ships.
There was no shore contact at any point. What was he doing?
Well, on one trip he had transferred cases of liquor from the
Malahat and *Principo* to small boats, but that did not make him
a rumrunner. Others did the rumrunning. His destination was
the high seas, and he returned from the high seas. No Canadian
law had been broken.

Captain G.A. Lilley had left the *Jessie* and at the time of the
commission hearing was in charge of the *Chris Moeller* which,
loaded with a total of fifteen thousand cases of whisky in Vancouver, was about to sail for Victoria to take on another five
thousand cases before setting out for San Blas, Mexico. It was
an unlikely destination; San Blas, a town of a few hundred inhabitants, had no port facilities and the harbour was navigable
only by vessels with a draft of less than six feet. Like Ensenada,
another frequently named destination, San Blas had no railroad
connection to the rest of Mexico. As far as the prospect of profit
went, the *Chris Moeller*'s intended sailing date had been well
chosen; there was no better time to arrive with liquor supplies
for California than just before Christmas. As far as the practicalities
went, an intended sailing date occurring when a commission
was focussing on false liquor clearances was unfortunate. In
spite of Captain Lilley's plea that putting to sea was how he
made his living, permission to sail was denied.

The commission finding that fraud, forgery and falsehood
were rampant in procuring customs clearances for fictitious des-

tinations to non-existent consignees came as no surprise. And it seemed most of the liquor held in bond in Vancouver and Victoria warehouses was not really in transit. Incoming shipments had stayed in storage for as long as nine months—awaiting purchase, presumably. The recommendations of the commission would not change the law—that was the business of Parliament—but they did pass a strong message to the rumrunning community.

The big rum traders, adept at reading messages that might cut their profits, acted swiftly. Before the ink on the royal commission recommendations was dry, British Columbia had lost its pre-eminent position as a supplier to the rum trade. The French possession of Tahiti would be the new supply point. Charges for bonding liquor on the Pacific island were moderate, the extra distances not impossibly great, and government regulations were more relaxed. Action followed the decision without a moment wasted. From warehouses all over Vancouver, trucks helped to bring forty thousand cases of liquor to Ballantyne Pier to be stowed on the Swedish ship *Falsterbe* bound for the Tahitian port of Papeete.

Coincidentally, it was on the day the new arrangement to use Tahiti was announced in the Vancouver newspapers, that the *Federalship* left Vancouver and steamed towards her fateful meeting with the coast guard cutters that forced her to make an unplanned detour to the San Francisco waterfront.

If the royal commission had brought one change in the operating methods of the rumrunners, the success of the coast guard brought another. The rum barons decided to send more ships to sea. Mother ships such as the *Malahat* were few. So few that keeping an eye on them was fairly easy. Using distributor boats that took cargo from the mother ships and then supplied liquor orders to shore-bound rumrunners made life more difficult for the coast guard. A single cutter could watch a single ship; many ships made choices necessary. Given that the coast guard had a limited number of ships available, only a limited number of ships could be watched at any time. With more rum traders about, some would inevitably escape to carry out their business unobserved.

The *Malahat*, a five-masted, wooden sailing ship of slightly over fifteen hundred tons, had been built for the lumber trade in 1917 and had later been modified by fitting auxiliary engines. When rumrunning had started off the west coast of North America, her combination of wind and engine power made her an ideal rum supply ship. As elusive as the Scarlet Pimpernel, she had evaded capture time after time. And each evasion had left the coast guard looking foolish. Looking foolish and feeling most frustrated.

But as she broke the drought brought on by the capture of the *Federalship*, the coast guard was determined to take her by any means necessary. Earlier, they had left ships well alone if found outside a twelve-mile limit. Closer inshore, warning rather than disabling shots were used to discourage rumrunners. In the case of the *Federalship*, taken by force outside normal limits, a judge had freed her, but there had been plenty of opinion that held seizure on the high seas to be proper when carried out to maintain the sanctity of the dry laws. The end justified the means. The law was a peculiar beast; you never could tell which way a judge would jump. If she could be caught, it was worth it to take the *Malahat*, wherever she was to be found, and then hand the resulting tangle to the courts to sort out. Since late in 1924, the Pacific fleet of the coast guard had been very successful in keeping captured Canadian rum ships off the high seas by enmeshing them in legal red tape.

So when the *Malahat* was found by the cutter *Shawnee* one hundred miles due west of Cape Conception, it was known that she had picked up her cargo in Tahiti, surmised that she had been the source of booze taken in three separate ambushes by prohibition agents on one night, and accepted that she was well outside legal search and seizure limits. No matter. The device of having too many ships at sea for the coast guard to adequately monitor had not worked this time. The chance of making a capture was too good to miss, and the cutters *Tamarac* and *Cahokia* were called up to assist. It would be three armed ships against one unarmed ship.

However, the single ship had the weather as an ally. A sudden gale stirred the ocean to a howling fury filling the air with driven water as spume from cresting waves mixed with sheets of driving rain. Watch-keepers in streaming oilskins stood on heaving decks, tasted salt water on their lips, shielded their half-closed eyes with their hands, and saw nothing. The search was next to impossible, but the coast guard cutters persisted. The weather had to improve. And it did. The gale dropped, the sea became calm, and the searchers anxiously waited for the visibility to get better. It failed to get better. Shifting banks of sea fog soon covered the ocean, and in them the *Malahat* ghosted silently away with all lights doused.

When she had been briefly visible, attempts to hit the *Malahat* with cannon fire had failed. If this was being under coast guard guns, it was not a very serious problem. Yet the persistence of the coast guard crews had turned the tap off again temporarily. One cutter, the *Cahokia*—the last to give up the fruitless chase— was 630 miles from the Californian coast when forced to turn back by dwindling fuel supplies. So much for twelve miles or one-hour's steaming distance from the coast as the fixed limit for search and seizure!

The chase over, life on the *Malahat* returned to its humdrum pattern. The chase had not been the stuff of high adventure; if any of the crew had gone to sea in the rum trade with romantic notions of a swashbuckling life, they had chosen the wrong ship. The old five-master was sadly neglected; spit and polish paid no dividends. Her liquor-stuffed holds were cavernous, her crew accommodations cramped and primitive. Men lived for months without privacy; personal appearance was nothing, clothes were washed in hard-to-lather sea water, if at all; a freshwater bath once a week was the most that could be expected. Boredom was the norm; entertainment was whatever sailors could provide for themselves. Prohibition, on a ship loaded with liquor, was strictly enforced; booze was for profit-making, not drinking. The ship sailed far from land for months, apparently fixed in place on an unchanging sea. Unchanging, that is, until a storm brewed to add cold, wet and general misery to the seemingly aimless voyage.

Much was made of the fact that the *Malahat* had failed to get rid of her last two thousand cases of liquor. But, even so, her voyage was far from having been a failure. She was carrying 18,000 cases of liquor, not 10,000 cases as first reported. That being so, 16,000 cases had been off-loaded at various points off the Pacific coast of the United States. So much for prohibition!

Early in November 1928, the coast guard, apparently having learned nothing from the *Federalship* affair and having failed to catch the *Malahat* the previous year, intercepted the steamship *L'Aquila* and called on her master to stop. As in the *Federalship* incident, the ship was about three hundred miles from the Californian coast and, being peacefully engaged on his owner's business on the high seas, her skipper saw no reason to obey. "Stop! What for? I'm on the high seas," he yelled through his megaphone. The captain of the coast guard cutter *Tamarac* applied gentle persuasion by means of a shot across the bows. It had no effect; the irate captain on the merchantman's bridge was not stopping for anyone. The roughness of the sea decided the cutter's captain that boarding was out of the question. Sensibly, he called for help and stayed close to the *L'Aquila*. When reinforcements arrived, warning shots were tried again. But still the merchantman ploughed doggedly on through the heavy seas. A deliberate shot from the cannon of one of the coast guard cutters hit the *L'Aquila* broadside on, denting the rusty iron sheathing of her hull. She stopped.

The charge justifying the arrest of the ship on the high seas was unique—it was piracy. Sure she had a load of liquor on board, but that was irrelevant. The ship had been operating on a provisional British certificate of registry; provisional and time-expired. Technically, the ship had no country. Therefore it was a pirate ship, amenable to the discipline of any nation without fear of upsetting anyone. The date on a ship's registration certificate is not visible to passing ships. From where did the captain of the *Tamarac* get his information? The answer is from officials in the American capital who made it their business to know of such things. It was from Washington that his orders to take the steamship had originated. There was reason, of a sort, behind the decision, and possibly a measure of spite. The *L'Aquila* was the *Federalship* renamed. The fuming figure on her bridge was Captain Stone.

For the second time, Captain Stuart S. Stone had his ship ignominiously towed into San Francisco Bay.

There were two aspects to the new American determination to have the prohibition laws obeyed. The first aspect was that there seemed to be no limit to the distance beyond the shore that coast guard cutters would act, in spite of international agreements. The second aspect was that there appeared to be no limit to the degree of force that would be used. It happened that on the Pacific coast no loss of life occurred because of coast guard gunfire. It was not so on the other coasts of the United States.

In March 1929, the *I'm Alone* was sighted in the Gulf of Mexico. She was outside the one-hour's steaming distance according to her captain; she was inside that distance according to the captain of the *Dexter*, the intercepting cutter. She was ordered to heave-to and refused. It was a familiar story to that point. But then the *Dexter* sheered off and the cutter *Wolcott* took over pursuit. The chase continued for two days and two nights, and for all of that time the ships were well out into international waters. The *Wolcott's* guns put several shells through the *I'm Alone's* rigging and then, after a final call to stop that drew no response, fired in earnest. After sixty or seventy hits by shells from the cutter's three-inch guns, punctuated by volleys of rifle fire, the *I'm Alone* sank. Her crew plunged into a sea growing increasingly rough and swam desperately for their lives. All were taken aboard the cutter. But for one of them it was too late. Leon Mainguy, boatswain, was dead when pulled from the water. The ship, her liquor and Mainguy were gone. The survivors, under arrest, were landed at New Orleans. A diplomatic storm was about to break.

Canada protested the sinking. There was a treaty in operation. Nothing in that treaty gave the United States the right to sink the ships of other nations on the high seas. And the sinking had been quite deliberate. No attempt had been made to merely disable the steering gear. Had there been a "hot and continuous pursuit," the coast guard might have had an excuse for taking a boat first seen within American waters. But the pursuit had not been continuous. The cutter *Dexter* had started the chase and had then handed it over to the cutter *Wolcott*. And the *Wolcott's* pursuit had not been continuous either; at one point she had broken away to examine a passing tanker. The United States government could hardly deny responsibility for the sinking. It accepted that Canada was due "honorary amends," but no hard cash. The shipping company wanted $50,000 compensation for the loss of the *I'm Alone*, Captain Randall, her master, wanted $25,000 for his abrupt loss of command, and the crew wanted $10,000 each for their various discomforts. They would not get it easily.

A joint Canadian-United States commission ruled on the matter—well after the end of prohibition. Canada got an apology from the United States along with $25,000 compensation—a total of $368,000 had been asked. The commission decided that the crew members of the *I'm Alone* had played no part in a scheme to smuggle liquor into the United States; they were employees hired to navigate the ship from place to place as directed. It followed, by reason of their non-participation in a criminal act, that they should be compensated for lost clothing and effects. And also for the wrong that had been done to them by casting them into the sea and then putting them in irons. Captain John T. Randall was awarded $6,906—slightly over one-quarter of the amount of his original demand. The crew members averaged about one-tenth of what they had demanded: the representative of John Williams, by that time deceased, was given $1,250; Jens Jansen got $1,098; James Barrett received an award of $1,032; Eddie Young was paid $999; Chesley Hobbs got $1,323; and Edward Fouchard received $965. The price of being dumped unceremoniously into the ocean and then fished out to be clapped in irons was remarkably low. Worst of all was the sum awarded to William Wordsworth, listed as now dead. His representative was awarded the magnificent sum of $57. Captain Randall, while expressing his disgust at the dismal amount of the compensation awarded, had something to say about what had happened to Wordsworth: "That lad died of the shock of his experience." Amanda Mainguy, the widow of Leon Mainguy, the member of the crew who lost his life when the *I'm Alone* was sunk, was awarded $10,185 for herself and her children. The ship's owners received nothing. For less than $50,000 the United States government got clear of the whole mess — far less than the cost of the ship and the lost liquor.

A second diplomatic incident occurred over the sinking of the *Josephine K* by the coast guard cutter *G-145* in January 1931. The location was different, off the New Jersey coast, but the story was familiar. A challenge, a call to halt, a refusal to do so because of a geographical position well outside the jurisdiction of the cutter, followed by swift retribution for having the temerity to refuse. The Canadian government's note to Washington protested such action being taken outside treaty limits and wondered, somewhat plaintively, whether the degree of violence used, which resulted in the killing of the *Josephine K*'s captain, William P. Cluett, was justified. In the usual way of the diplomatic world, formal acknowledgement of the note was made, and there the matter rested for a while. But not for as long as usual. The United States government wanted this new case kept separate from the *I'm Alone* arbitration.

Arbitration is a slow business and expensive business. Governments must win—or at least save face, and arbitration gives no such guarantee. The United States government moved to keep control in its own hands. In less than a year, a settlement was made. The escalating violence of coast guard action was evidence of its inability to put an end to the trade of rumrunning. It would never end while the unenforceable Eighteenth Amendment was a part of the American constitution. Political action had brought the amendment into being; only political action could bring it to an end.

9
THE RESURRECTION OF JOHN BARLEYCORN

Passersby kept a wary eye on the man weaving down the street and timed their progress to avoid his errant lurches. A seedy looking individual, poorly dressed and underfed, he was determined to walk straight. But there was a problem; his feet seemed to have a perverse will of their own. He muttered to himself as his feet tangled and one shoulder struck a rough brick wall. He pawed at the wall and tried to move on. A patrolling police officer raised a tolerant eyebrow and moved in to assist. It was no use. The drunk was beyond the help that a steadying hand could provide. The police officer, believing that a long sleep in a jail cell was the only cure for the staggering man's ailment, sent for the paddy wagon to cart him off. The drunk was incensed. He roused himself to make a threat. "Repeal's here," he hiccuped, "and if you take me to jail, I'll sue you. Sure as shooting, I'll sue you." It was a threat made a touch too soon; the repeal of national prohibition was due to take effect on the following day.

It seemed no time at all since evangelist Billy Sunday had symbolically buried John Barleycorn in Norfolk, Virginia as prohibition began. No one had any doubt on that day that the traditional symbol of the liquor trade, put under the sod by constitutional amendment, had gone forever. But they were wrong. Less than thirteen years later, "that bibulous and notorious character, John Barleycorn" returned from the grave in triumph.

The Volstead Act, said an irate senator, was an idiocy.

Commercial breweries had been closed, and millions of little breweries had sprung up in homes all over America to replace them. Drink purchases were now by the case when they had formerly been by the glass. The coast guard were pointing to increased liquor seizures as a measure of their success, yet in the past three years the amount of illicit liquor coming in from Canada alone had increased by 75 percent.

And the methods of the prohibition agencies were deplorable. The bible, prayerbook and temperance tract the senator could stomach as means of persuading people not to drink; the lash, the prison, the gun and the bludgeon—the tools of fanatical bigots bent on having their way—he could not. The senator's claim of the use of excessive force sounded extreme—the lash, the prison, the gun, the bludgeon! Yet, with the exception of the lash, the senator was able to cite incidents in the previous year that rooted his claims in fact. A coast guard ship off the Florida coast, firing at a fleeing rumrunner, had landed shells on houses along the shore. A woman in Illinois had been killed as she tried to help her husband who had been knocked senseless by prohibition agents. The mother of ten children had been sentenced to imprisonment for life under what had become known as the "life-for-a-pint" law. These were American citizens. Was the control of alcoholic drink so important as to excuse these barbaric acts?

In 1928 Herbert Hoover became president of the United States. The problem was his to solve. Predictably, he set up a commission with a mandate that would not conflict with his own view that prohibition was good, but would suggest ways of improving the application of the law. It was not all smooth sailing. Some commissioners were scathing about enforcement methods. Some had the temerity to suggest an easing of the laws relating to alcohol—to hack away at the prohibition laws. But discipline prevailed. The commissioners' final report made few positive suggestions and firmly opposed any significant change to the prohibition laws.

The contrast between the early critical comments of the commissioners and their final conclusion was the subject of a sardonic verse printed in the *New York World*:

Prohibition is an awful flop.
We like it. It can't stop what its meant to stop.
We like it.
It's left a trail of graft and slime,
It don't prohibit worth a dime,
It's filled our land with vice and crime,
Nevertheless we're for it.

Prohibition was not going to go by government action. But when the stock exchange crashed in 1929, there was a change of emphasis. Was prohibition so important? Possibly there might be economic advantages to bringing it to an end. American breweries and distilleries would need workers. Farmers would benefit from a renewed demand for grain. Governments would regain the huge liquor taxation incomes they had once had. Perhaps that would bring income tax rates down. It was all very simplistic, but very attractive.

In 1933, Franklin Delano Roosevelt, former supporter of prohibition, ran for the presidency against Herbert Hoover and won. His views on prohibition had changed. During the campaign, he was asked if he would bring back beer if elected. He said he would—and raise several hundred million dollars by taxing it. The audience cheered. Such enthusiasm for taxation did not suggest a bright future for prohibition. The writing was on the wall, and the politicians took notice.

Even before Franklin Roosevelt was inaugurated, a proposed Twenty-third Amendment to the constitution—a prohibition killer—had already been sent to the individual states for ratification. Before prohibition began, thirteen opposing states could have kept the nation wet; and when the time came to vote on repeal, thirteen opposing states could keep the nation dry. On the fifth day of December 1933, Utah became the thirty-sixth state to accept the Twenty-first Amendment. The minimum number of states required for the repeal of prohibition had been reached. Prohibition was dead. John Barleycorn lived again.

Between the death of one and the resurrection of the other, there was confusion as states struggled to cope with the new situation. But ardent drinkers living near the Canadian border were not confused. They headed north to stock up to the limit deemed reasonable for a returning adult American citizen—one quart of liquor, duty-free, and one hundred taxable dollars'-worth in addition. And when American citizens could carry their own liquor across the border, rumrunning was dead. No longer would the adventurous be drawn by the easy life that made normal employment and normal wages unattractive—if, in 1933, employment of any kind could be found.

But the end of rumrunning was not as clear-cut as the Utah vote suggested. The end would came for rumrunners when individuals and companies saw no further hope of profit. Johnny Schnarr, owner of his own boat and carrier for whoever was willing to pay, ended his last trip on the second day of April, 1933—eight months before the Utah vote. His pride and joy, the *Revuocnav* (Vancouver written backwards), was now an embarrassment. Few buyers were likely to want a boat fifty-six feet long, capable of forty knots when both her 860-horsepower engines were at full throttle and guzzling gas at a rate of 120 gallons an hour. Schnarr had made some money in his rumrunning career but others had profited more than he. The United States merchants of illicit booze to whom he had delivered sixty thousand cases of liquor, for example. Canada itself, perhaps. The sixty thousand cases Schnarr had carried from Canada to the United States had played a part in boosting the Canadian economy. But it was over and done with. What does an ex-rumrunner do? Johnny Schnarr tried logging, but the sea water was too thick in his veins to give him peace. In time he settled down as a commercial fisherman.

Other ships and other operators clung to the doomed trade as long as it was possible to do so. Off San Francisco, the *Ryou II* had spent the first days of August 1933 under the watchful eye of the coast guard cutter *Cahokia*. It was the final incident of surveillance in the rumrunning boat's career. On the tenth of the month, still with seven hundred cases of liquor in her hold, she was recalled to Vancouver. Pausing only to transfer her remaining load to a mother ship, the *Ryou II* splashed northward at a stolid six knots and arrived home on August 28. At the offices of Consolidated Exporters, the crew was paid off. Fraser Miles, the *Ryou II*'s radio operator and general dogsbody, received $1,500 for ten months of hard work and was well content. In total, he had been paid $2,400 for a seagoing career of nearly two years. As he reckoned it, he had helped handle 15,000 cases of liquor at sixteen cents a case. At the Seattle price of $200 a case, the sale of twelve cases would have paid for his two years of effort. Loading from mother ships, moving away, and waiting for pick-up boats from the American shore, and repeating the process without apparent end, had had its exciting moments, but not many. Perhaps the boredom of the task is best expressed in a few words from his book, *Slow Boat on Rum Row*. "We drifted from November eighteenth to December the tenth. Quite ignored by all . . . ." Bored or not, ill-paid or not, Fraser Miles put his rumrunning days to better use than most. The money he earned paid for an education that formed the basis of a successful career in electrical engineering. Ironically, the money earned by helping to make a mockery of American laws was spent at an American college.

In May 1933, milking the cash cow of rumrunning to its last drops, the liquor supply ship *Mogul* left Vancouver for the extreme northwestern end of the Mexican coast. There, five miles off-shore, she relieved the *Malahat* and opened shop. As Mexico stuck to the internationally agreed three-mile limit, there was no question of illegality. But that is not to say that the United States authorities were uninterested. Constantly, a coast guard cutter hovered by to head off any American vessels that might wish to deal. But it was a minor inconvenience. As night fell, speedboats pulled alongside the *Mogul*, loaded, and raced for American beaches to put expensive cargoes ashore. It was easy to make the coast guard look foolish.

But there came a time when the crew members of the *Mogul* were jerked out of their affable impudence. Unknown to anyone on board, the *Mogul's* owners had been negotiating with Washington. Within miles of the United States lay a rich cargo of liquor that could not legally be landed. Prohibition was about to end, and when it ended there would be no bar to importation. The owners tried to apply a dash of common sense—to their own advantage, of course. Let the liquor land and be kept in bond until the repeal of the Eighteenth Amendment, they asked. Their approach to the United States government was somewhat cavalier: rather than sending a representative to Washington, they sent a telegram. The telegram said too much. The *Mogul's* owners had suggested that allowing the liquor to land would put paid to smuggling. They owned the only large supply ship then on the coast. Remove its cargo and it was unlikely that any other company could arrange financing and shipping of another load within six months. The United States government read the message as a threat: allow the cargo to land and be held in bond or we shall smuggle it ashore in spite of any efforts you might make. To the amazement of the *Mogul*'s crew, seven United States cutters suddenly steamed into position around the ship and navy airplanes circled overhead. The reason for the sudden activity, the crew learned from news broadcasts made by Californian radio stations.

It was a a brief interlude. Having put the *Mogul*'s owners firmly in their place, the American government withdrew its impressive show of force, and the *Mogul* was left in peace.

On December 5, 1933, the Eighteenth Amendment was repealed and the ship's captain received orders to shut up shop. In the holds were fifty-four thousand cases of liquor containing two hundred different brands. The crew sat and waited. And waited. And still waited. Each day they expected orders to weigh anchor and head for some port where the cargo would be discharged. They waited five months in all, and when they unloaded it was at Ensenada, Mexico, a few miles away.

Then the ship sailed home to Vancouver in ballast. The *Mogul*'s return passage was slow, but there was no need to hurry. The ship's reason for existence had disappeared. All the owners now wanted was a good price from whoever wished to buy her. Ships that had raked in fortunes were now a liability. The well had filled to the brim and suddenly emptied. Seamen were now finding it difficult to squeeze a cent of wages out of penurious owners. Suing for back wages hardly helped. In some instances the sale of the devalued vessels brought in insufficient money to square the account.

"Hurry home, baby, with the dough." The fervent words of the wife of one of the owners solved the problem of what the reconditioned vessel on the slipway was to be called. When she was launched, the crack of a champagne bottle on her bow made it official. The *Hurry Home* slipped into the water to begin her rumrunning career. But the end of prohibition was near and her glory days were over almost before they began. Soon the crew was owed a total of almost $10,000, and the courts said that they should be paid. Should be, but by whom? And with what?

The *Hurry Home*, under British registry, was owned by business-men in the United States. The ship was seized and offered for sale. At a public auction the highest bid for the ninety-foot vessel, not many years before fitted with a new engine, was $1,200. She was withdrawn from sale. The crew could whistle for their wages.

Two famous rumrunning ships went back to the tasks for which they had been designed. The *Stadacona*, (later renamed *Moonlight Maid*) had once been a luxury yacht and after prohibition's end again became the pampered toy of a rich owner. The *Malahat*, designed for the timber trade, returned to it. But decline was inevitable for both ships.

In 1941 the *Moonlight Maid* was bought by a salvage com-pany and, after her graceful bowsprit had been removed and a more effective propeller fitted, became a tug. Perhaps not a very effec-tive tug, for only a year later the one-time yacht was bought by the U.S government for use as a cargo ship supplying army bases in Alaska and the Aleutians. In 1948 the *Moonlight Maid*'s final owners broke her up, after gutting her superstructure by fire as she lay beached near a Seattle park. It was a sad end to a fine ship.

The old *Malahat* fared even worse when her glory days in the rum trade were done. Within a year the old ship, headed for Vancouver with a cargo of logs, hit a reef in dense fog and was holed in the bow. There were repairs to be done, debts piled up and among them was the sum of $1,926 owed to the crew. A court ordered the *Malahat* to be sold for a minimum of $2,500. Old as she was that made her a reasonable buy, considering she had $1,500 worth of spare parts on board and tanked fuel worth another $1,000. Again in use, her career resumed its downward path. One skipper, once her captain during the hal-cyon days of rumrunning, found the owners had removed a mast as he slept, to increase her capacity for a deck cargo of logs. Other men, hired to command her, took one look at her state and refused to put to sea. In 1943, the *Malahat*, once a proud ocean-going vessel, came to the end of her useful life when sunk in Barkley Sound.

When the *Malahat* sank, prohibition was a memory and the rumrunners had faded into a wider world. While they lasted, the rum ships, debris of a unique era, were a reminder of times past. But now they are gone and, for the most part, the men who played leading roles in that era are gone. Could it happen

Rumrunner *Stadacona*, as the yacht *Moonlight Maid*. (*photo courtesy of the Vancouver Maritime Museum*)

again? Does history repeat itself?

The total prohibition of intoxicating drinks is—to put it very mildly—unlikely. But what of rumrunning? Can it exist without prohibition? Yes it can. Rumrunning had a long history in North America before prohibition gained its precarious footing—and it still exists. In 1992 Canadian customs officers made over twenty-two thousand seizures of liquor being smuggled into Canada from the United States. Some of the seizures were of single bottles being smuggled into Canada by Canadians trying to avoid high liquor taxes at home; but not all. The criminal element was also hard at work demonstrating that declaring false destinations for liquor in transit still works.

Claims have been made that during the second quarter of 1993 a company known as the West Africa Trading Company bought fifty-four thousand bottles of liquor in New Hampshire for shipment to Nigeria. The bottles traveled by a circuitous route: first to Montreal and then on to Halifax, Nova Scotia for ocean shipment to Africa. A cargo delivered to Halifax would be no nearer to Nigeria than if it had been shipped to the port of Boston, an hour's journey from the bottling plant. Why waste money on such a complicated journey? The answer is simple: most of the liquor never reaches Halifax but is sold to the drinking establishments of Montreal and Toronto.

The New Hampshire shipments may be a drop in the bucket. From Kentucky, California, Oregon and Washington, following routes that cross Canadian soil, scores of similar liquor shipments have been made to declared African destinations. In a manner reminiscent of prohibition days, few of the two hundred thousand cases of liquor thought to be involved have ever arrived at their announced destination. The liquor enters Canada and stays in Canada—illegally.

Shades of the "good old days." Prohibition! Who needs it? North American rumrunning still lives. But that is another story.

BIBLIOGRAPHY

Books

Allyn, Stan. *Top Deck Twenty! Best West Coast Sea Stories!* (Portland: Binford & Mort, 1989).

Campbell, Robert A. *Demon Rum or Easy Money.* Government Control of Liquor in British Columbia from Prohibition to Privatization (Ottawa: Carelton University Press, 1991).

Cashman, Sean Dennis. *Prohibition: The Lie of the Land* (New York: The Free Press, 1981).

Clark, Norman H. *Deliver Us from Evil: An Interpretation of American Prohibition* (New York: Norton & Co., 1976).

_____ . *The Dry Years* (Seattle: The University of Washington Press, 1988).

Gibbs, James A. *Pacific Graveyard* (Portland: Binfords & Mort, 1964).

Gray, James H. *Bacchanalia Revisited: Western Canada's Boozy Skid to Social Disaster* (Saskatoon: Western Producer Prairie Books, n.d.).

Greene, Ruth. *Personality Ships of British Columbia* (West Vancouver: Marine Tapestry Publications, 1969).

Hallowell, Gerald A. *Prohibition in Ontario, 1919-1923* (Ottawa: Ontario Historical Society Research Publication No. 2, 1972).

Hunt, C. W. *Booze, Boats and Billions: Smuggling Liquid Gold* (Toronto: McClelland and Stewart, 1988).

Kobler, John. *Ardent Spirits: The Rise and Fall of Prohibition* (London: Michael Joseph, 1974).

Marshall, Don. *Oregon Shipwrecks* (Portland: Binfords & Mort, 1984).

Miles, Fraser. *Slow Boat on Rum Row* (Madeira Park: Harbour Publishing, 1992).

Morrison, James H. and James Moreira, eds. *Tempered by Rum* (Porters Lake, N.S.: Pottersfield Press, 1988).

Newman, Peter C. *The Canadian Establishment, Vol. I* (Toronto: McLelland & Stewart, 1975).

Newsome, Eric. *The Case of the Beryl G* (Victoria: Orca Book Publishers, 1989).

Parker, Marion and Robert Tyrrell. *Rumrunner: The Life and Times of Johnny Schnarr* (Victoria: Orca Book Publishers, 1988).

Richardson, David. *Pig War Islands*, (East Sound, Washington: Orcas Publishing Company, 2d. ed. 1990).

Sinclair, A. *Era of Excess: A Social History of the Prohibition Movement* (New York: Harper & Row, 1962).

Starkins, E. "Rum Running." In *Rain Coast Chronicles First Five,* edited by Howard White (Madeira Park, B.C.: Harbor Publishing, 1976).

Waters, Harold. *Smugglers of Spirits: Prohibition and the Coast Guard Patrol* (New York: Hastings House, 1971).

White, James Seeley. *Diving For Northwest Relics* (Portland: Binford & Mort, 1979).

Magazine Articles

Clark, Norman H. "Roy Olmstead, A Rumrunning King on Puget Sound." *Pacific Northwest Quarterly* (July, 1963).

Kelly, L.V. "Rum-Running Was Rough." *British Columbia Magazine, The Vancouver Province* (April 2, 1955).

Lonsdale, Captain A. L. "Rumrunners on Puget Sound." *American West* (November, 1972).

Rannie, William F. "Old, Big, Colourful: The Distilling Industry." *Canadian Geographical Journal* (Dec. 1976 / Jan. 1977).

Newspapers

Various editions of:
  Astoria Evening Budget
  Beach Resort News, Lincoln, Oregon
  Bellingham American
  Bellingham Evening News
  Bellingham Herald,
  Portland Oregonian
  Seattle Post-Intelligencer
  Seattle Times
  Vancouver *Province*
  Vancouver Sun
  Victoria Daily Colonist

INDEX